THE DOWNRIVER
HORSESHOE

ST LEN TIME
PUBLISHING

STORIES BY:
SCOTT MILES

The stories in this collection first appeared (some in slightly different form) in these publications: "When You're the Mailman" in *The Cimarron Review,* "Mt. Trashmore" in *LIT Magazine,* "Freezer Burn" in *Atticus Review,* "Fungoo's Hockshop" in *Beloit Fiction Journal,* "Crash Where You Land" in *Storyglossia,* "Paddy Wagon" in *Crime Factory,* "Altoona" in *The Oyez Review,* "Stripped" in *Avatar Review,* "One More Try" in *The Pebble Lake Review,* "Erwin's Main Attraction" in *Needle: A Magazine of Noir,* "Losing Focus" in *The MacGuffin.*

"Losing Focus" (*The MacGuffin*) and "Freezer Burn" (*Atticus Review*) were subsequently nominated for the Pushcart Prize.

Published by:
Stolen Time Publishing
6933 N. Kedzie
Chicago, IL 60645

ISBN-10: 0692222693
ISBN-13: 978-0692222690

Cover and Back Cover Design by: **Marcio Cabral**
Back Cover Photo: **Kenneth Bailey**

THE DOWNRIVER HORSESHOE draws its stories from the landscapes and people of the industrial, south side of Metro Detroit called Downriver. It is Americana with a gritty, blue-collar twist—filled with quirky, rough-hewn characters like Duke Peterson, a retired cookie-truck driver who, at the behest of his nasty, invalid wife, has to hock his grandfather's old shotguns to make rent; there is George Rimbaud, a morally confused mailman who continually crosses the line and intertwines his life (and sex life) with people along his route; and also Simon Touhy, a young man who falls in love with a prosthetic leg found at his worksite on Mt. Trashmore, a landfill converted to public ski slope. With the luck and pride of Downriver at their side, these men march on, making the best decisions they can in an area that can be bleak and beautiful and dangerous on the same block.

Praise for **THE DOWNRIVER HORSESHOE**:

Every story in **THE DOWNRIVER HORSESHOE** is full of secrets, and so many of the lines keep surprising me. The way Scott Miles sees the world is fresh and effortless, like a kid coming across a new animal he's never seen before. What do you name it? How do you describe its sound? That's the experience—except with strippers, suicide, brutality, and a whole lot of pain.

—Anthony Neil Smith, author of **ALL THE YOUNG WARRIORS**

Scott Miles's writing is funny and dark, often on the same page. His compelling characters and original stories make **THE DOWNRIVER HORSESHOE** a must-read collection. Highly recommended.

—Steve Weddle, author of **COUNTRY HARDBALL**

Good writers know how to flip a phrase, coin a simile. A great writer, like Scott Miles, makes other writers want to steal from him. Visiting and revisiting Scott's stories are like hitchhiking barefooted on the side of the road. As you scan for signposts, you cut the soles of your feet on shards of shattered glass. The jagged edges sting, prick, and splinter your skin, and you're sure you'll never make it to the ball on time. But once you get past the pain, you're amazed by how the pieces fit and form a whole—not of a magic slipper—but a steel-tipped work boot made of grit and kerosene.

—Dan Cafaro, Founder and Publisher, **ATTICUS BOOKS**

Great thanks and respect to:

The literary magazines and editors for first publishing these stories, the good people in the Fiction Writing Department at Columbia College Chicago, Marc Paoletti, Jeff Mikos, Paul Grens, Matt Stabley, Julia Borcherts, Mary-Beth Hoerner, Karen Zemanick, Brandi Kleinert-Larsen, Matt Larsen, Rob Duffer, the Downriver crew (Rathbone, Jay, Nay, T-bag, Moletown), Marcio Cabral, Sean Menick, my parents, my brother Dave, my sister Kim, my wife Larisa, and my two daughters, Selma & Dina. You all rule.

THE DOWNRIVER HORSESHOE
STORIES BY SCOTT MILES

When You're the Mailman

Today the old coot answers the door in pajamas fit for an infant, sporting whiskers like a gray dust broom. By now he usually tells me he wants to die, that dying would be to his benefit. But he doesn't tell me that story today. Instead he grunts sullenly, nostrils flaring.

He must be on the final slide, I think. I wish I could help. I wish I could hold this man's thin-skinned hand to the lip of the grave, show him where he needs to go, and then give him a little shove into the hole. But I can't do that. I like the old fella too much. I fork over his mail and the cellophane window crinkles under hand:

Mr. Raymond Johansen
4359 Polk St.
Melvindale, MI 48122

"Your mailbox is broke, Mr. Johansen," I say.

This itchy postal uniform is tight. It's hugging my crotch.

"I know that, boy," he says. "The god damn key broke off in the lock yesterday. Everything breaks off in the cold like this."

"Tell me about it." I like to sympathize, my breath blooming out like a fog machine.

"Next thing you know my god damn leg'll break off!" He lifts his brittle leg and gives it a twist and a 'crack!' He then laughs through a jaundiced mouth, a pestilent cough.

"Just the same, I'd look into getting that mailbox fixed."

"Why is that?" The old man is confounded.

"I don't mind coming up to your door and giving you your mail for a couple of days," I say. "But I'm really not allowed to do that."

"Why's that?"

"U.S. Postal policy. I have to put a 'stop' on your mail and report to my supervisor that your mailbox is broken. And she's a stickler for rules. She's a real bitch."

"Your supervisor, eh?" Mr. Johansen grabs his stubbly chin while his face turns a reddish shade of deviant. "What's she look like?"

"She's got a good set of tits," I explain. "Tall. Dark hair. Black."

"Black?" he says. "Never mind!" Mr. Johansen's shar-pei-like face scrunches up odiously. Born in a different time this man.

"Come on, Mr. Johansen."

"What?"

"You never had a hankering for black tail?"

"Get the hell off my property!"

"Ok, ok." I step off his porch. "But, don't forget the mailbox."

"Jesus fucking Christ, I'll look into it."

"Have a good day!"

"A good day," he says calmly and stalls to thumb through the mail. Bills, sweepstakes applications, coupons that he'll study for half a day before throwing them into a little basket he keeps on his kitchen table. "Good fucking day to die, that's what it is." He looks at me again, serious and stern like a petrified tree. "It's always something, isn't it George?" he says on the sly.

"Indeed it is, Mr. Johansen."

The door slams shut. I peek in through the door window and see him set down the mail, a cup of tea steeping on his kitchen table. Mr. Johansen's been like this since I've been on this route. He's a real bastard and he's always angry like a nest of wet wasps. He's too sharp for the asylum, yet too crazy to make a difference in life. We get along very well. We have an understanding. Still, it'd be nice if I could help him find his grave. He says he wants to die but no one's helping. Why shouldn't I help? I'm a government employee, aren't I?

Mr. Johansen catches me peering into his home and then flips me the bird. I smile and wave, then jerk my thumb back and say, "Get that mailbox fixed Mr. Johansen!"

The mail must continue.

Torre's house is as solid as a bar when I'm bored and need a drink after work. He's always got good beer in the fridge, or wine. French. Californian. Red. White. Every week I bring him the junk mail I've either forgotten to deliver or specifically put on the side for him. Mostly credit card applications and bills. Torre fills them out with the recipient's name, scribbles in some information and sends them back. He does his homework and memorizes social security numbers from old bills. He's gotten a few cards and always spends as much as he can the first day, then tosses the card into the Rouge River.

Torre and I have an understanding, too. I bring the applications and bills and he lets me drink his beer and wine. I've known Torre for three years now.

We usually get tipsy and talk about the books on his bookshelf, which is an impressive collection he inherited from his father. From philosophy to classical literature. Schopenhauer. Dostoevski. Vonnegut. Torre's old man was a lit professor in Ann Arbor. I guess he wrote a few science fiction books, too. He kicked the bucket early. Emphysema. Great word: emphysema. But it's a bad disease. His father left him and his mother a fortune. Torre's mother still lives in Ann Arbor. She also teaches at the University of Michigan.

Sometimes Torre and I talk about his old lady, Candice, who abandoned the house one dull summer day and never came back. Just up and left him with an infant child that isn't even his. Torre is white, Candice is white, but the baby is a little black boy. His name is Otis.

Otis usually sits in his crib, which has wooden bars and looks like a topless bird cage. I keep waiting for him to fly out. Sometimes Otis stands and waits there for an hour, always looking out at Torre and I.

Cute as a tater bug that kid. Wide eyes, quiet as hell, and he just stares at you. Not that dumb thick glazed stare, either. It's like Otis knows something you don't.

Torre opens up the door and I hand him a stack of mail.

"What's up, Torre?"

"Nada," he says and slides aside. "You stayin' long, George?" He then spits out onto the snowy ground. Torre is tall and lanky, legs like a scare crow, ruddy cheeks.

"For a beer or two."

"'Cause I gotta get some loot and run errands. Can you watch Otis for a little bit?"

"Sure, what the hell?"

I walk in behind Torre and then make tracks over to Otis, who smells like baby powder and sour milk. I cup Otis' little black head, the curls underneath my hands like a spindle of dark silk. I pull his head gently back and look into his eyes and say:

"Otis, it's me and you tonight punk! You up for that?"

"Gahhh."

"That's right. Gahhhh."

"Gahhh."

"Is the gahhhh in the fridge?" I ask.

"Hmmmm?" His eyes are watery, deep blue. Otis shakes the rattle in his hand.

"It is? Great. I'll just help myself to one, eh?"

Otis gives me a questioning look. He is two-years old and must really like that crib because he doesn't leave it much. I pick him up for a minute because I like to pick up kids. Who doesn't? His diaper crinkles and I sniff it to make sure he doesn't need changing.

Meanwhile Torre is rustling around in his bedroom. I hear him faintly over the television, which is tuned to some horrible Lifetime movie. Something about "rape" and stars the girl from Family Ties. Not the hot one either. The dumpy one. Tina Yothers.

"I'll be back in about an hour," Torre says.

"What do I feed this little runt? Burritos or pizza or something?" I kiss Otis on his warm skull with the brunt of my mouth. Soon, he'll be old like Mr. Johansen, leathery and cold. I wouldn't think Mr. Johansen's head is warm and soft like Otis'.

"He still eats baby food, you know that, George," Torre says, looking for his keys.

"Ok."

"The food's in the cupboard."

Torre then leaves without much adieu. Probably out to look for his wife. Poor sap.

Torre's been tracking down his wife for months now. He thinks she's in Las Vegas. She used to be a stripper here in Detroit, over at the Atlantis on Fort Street. That's where he met Candice, and by his reasoning, Vegas is where all the dancers go when things get really bad. It's like Mecca for desperate, out-of-work strippers.

From what I understand, Las Vegas isn't Candice's kind of town. She's a losable sort and Vegas is full of quacks and miscreants. Americana exhausted. Fleets of old ladies with dark visors covering their pink eyes. Old men with weak tickers, plaid pants. Imagine Candice in the middle of it all, losing her money on a broken roulette wheel, her abusive boyfriend at home snorting cocaine, waiting for her to return with clenched fists.

Next thing I know, I'm drooling on myself and waking up from a fatigued and drunken nap. Re-runs of Tom and Jerry are on the television screen. The ones where you can only see the legs of the black maid, who is swatting a broom at both Tom and Jerry. Otis is on the couch next to me, sleeping in his fuzzy pajamas, curled up like a pill bug. The gleaming cadence of numbers on the VCR says 12:32am.

I put Otis in his crib and fumble through Torre's mail. It's an old habit. I see pamphlets for a round-trip ticket to Las Vegas, a letter from the IRS, a collection agency from Lansing. Address Service Requested.

I've been a mailman for twelve years now. I like it. Always have. It's how I met Torre. I delivered mail to his house while he worked from his home. He's a graphic designer who gave me beer when I needed it most. I've always held him in high regard for this.

Delivering mail gives me time to think, walk through old neighborhoods, and fantasize about the lonely housewives in Detroit. I like the brief interludes with the people, too. You get so much more from people you only see every day for 10 seconds rather than those you spend your whole lifetime knowing, like family or old friends. You know what to expect. The relationship is much more satisfying, less daunting.

Delivering mail has brought me closer to humanity. I even meet women. For a while, I was seeing a lady on a route I had in Dearborn. Her name was Lydia Shortridge, 1256 W. Cherry Hill. I had only seen her from a distance. When I left her porch and got two or three houses down, she would come out and open the lid of her mailbox, always giving me a look. From down the street, she was attractive. She had a thin face, ruffles of dark hair.

As I approached her door one summer afternoon, Lydia opened the door with a vodka and OJ in one hand, the phone in the other, a cigarette dangling from her mouth. She was in skimpy lingerie and talking to her husband, quietly berating him for not coming home that previous night. She stood and waited with her shoulder propping the screen door open, that glint of boredom in her eyes. When I got closer, I noticed she was indeed thin but had an undercarriage like a broken-down Chevy, a dry scalp, and wore a little too much make-up.

When I handed her the mail, she waved me in with it, silently, hastily. I stepped in, dropped my bag and stood while she left the room to refreshen her OJ. Feeling very comfortable, I stripped down to my boxers, made myself a drink and watched television while she argued with her husband, Ron. I caught little snippets of conversation while she paced back and forth in her kitchen.

"You rotten bastard, I don't know why I ever—"

"Why don't you go fuck your—"

"Don't bother coming home!"

From that day on it was a brainless love affair. Sex for the sake of sex. We were the same age, 36, but she was years ahead of me in some other life I would never understand. I've never been married and never really knew my parents. I have no concept of family or wife or the dysfunctional life therein. I don't have anybody except for my foster mother, Torre, and a few distant cousins I still keep in touch with.

The act with Lydia went on for months. I would drop by her house for a quick lay and a stiff drink. Sometimes we'd talk about her husband, how lonely she was, how much she wanted a different life. But then fall came and I changed routes. The leaves dropped to the ground, waxy and yellow, the color of burnt yams. I never saw Lydia outside of my route, and I couldn't just show up for no reason. Therefore, I never saw her again, with or without my uniform. It was a simple equation.

Soon thereafter, Randall Feverson was handed the route on a silver fucking platter, and who better to take over with Lydia than Randall Feverson? The guy couldn't get laid in a whorehouse with a fistful of cash. In the locker room after the first day of his new route, while pulling on his thin beaten socks, he told me and everyone else about some bombshell he'd met and how she'd seduced him.

"What's her name?" I asked, though I already knew the answer.

"Some busty brunette named Lydia. I guess she's divorcing her husband, Ron."

Two months later, Randall told me that he was in love and that Lydia moved in with him. I shook his hand and congratulated him. I never told him about our sex affair. I suppose you could say it was noble of me, but I just didn't care. I didn't want anything to do with Lydia. She was a bit of a basket case.

The door opens as I'm heating up the pizza Otis and I ordered earlier. It's Torre.

"You want some pizza?" I ask.

"No, thanks," Torre says softly, eyes strained and demeanor shaken, possibly drunk.

He drops his keys in the drawer. The keys dance in a mess of outdated restaurant coupons while Torre fishes a beer from the fridge and walks into the living room. I grab my slice from the oven and follow him.

"I gotta go to Vegas, George."

"How the hell did you find her?"

"One of the escort pages on the internet," he says. "She changed her name to Trisha."

I wipe pizza grease on my jeans. "What are you gonna say to Trisha? Or should I say 'Trasha'?"

"I don't know."

I munch on my slice, the tip and crust are warm, crisp, the pepperoni is sweating grease, but the dough is cold in the middle. Torre gets up and looks out the window.

"Can you stay with Otis while I go out there?" He pleads this to the window pane, his back to me. Torre then turns and gives me the hard-luck look. "I can't bring him along."

I'm quite happy to be there for Torre in his time of need.

"Sure. It's not a good idea to expose Otis to Vegas this early," I say. "Seeing all those lights and neon would fuck with his mind. Either that or he'd get on that baccarat table and clean the town out. You'd guys would be rich."

Torre paces the floor like he didn't hear me. "I don't know what she'd do if she saw him."

"Maybe she'd want to come back?"

"I don't want her back," he says. "She's a whore now. Professionally speaking."

"Then why go out there? Why not forget her?"

"It's not that easy."

"When do you leave?"

"Tomorrow night."

"I'll come by after work and drive you to the airport."

As I leave Torre's house, I'm greeted by indigestion and a yellow, crescent moon, which hangs in the sky like an infected toenail.

Back at my place, I get lonely and wish I had love problems like Torre. At times like this, I wish I was in Lydia's bed so I could hear her talk about her husband. It was tedious and redundant, but it always soothed me when she bitched about Ron, because, deep down, she really loved him. The relationship made her life complicated and worthwhile.

The next day, I knock on Mr. Johansen's door and I'm startled to find a stranger answer. He's big, burly, wears a tight tee shirt, and sports a nose like a bruised rutabaga.

"Where's Mr. Johansen?" I ask.

The man pauses. "I'm afraid Ray passed away last night," he says with voice like gravel caught in a garbage disposal. I space out for a moment. A junkyard comes to mind and I wonder if we can use Mr. Johansen for spare parts. Surely the best parts of him are still alive. I'd like to tear the crankiness and wit out from underneath his hood.

"What happened?"

"He's been dying for years," he says matter-of-factly. "He's been on heart medication. Angina pectoris. He passed in his sleep."

"Who are you?"

"I'm the landlord. I came over to fix his leaky sink this morning."

He points to his metal toolbox on the floor. There's a big heavy wrench that sits on top of the lid, drizzled with white paint. This is what happens when you're the mailman. You find out that people live and die during the day, during your route. You find out that landlords come over to fix things. That lonely housewives yearn for a better life. That graphic freelancers wish their slutty wives would come back from Vegas.

"Here's his mail." I hand the guy a sordid bundle of useless mail. I begin to walk away and then turn around before he closes the door.

"While you're here, I'd fix that mailbox of his, too. It's been broken for a few days."

The landlord nods and waves the stack of mail at me. The door closes with a light clasp, certainly not the way Mr. Johansen would've slammed it shut.

On my way over to Torre's, I contemplate stopping at Randall Feverson's house to say hello to Lydia. I have yet more yearning to involve myself in someone else's tragedies and sordid love affairs.

But I don't. I realize the only person I need is Otis. Otis will have all the answers.

I knock on Torre's door and hear a high-pitched but muffled "Come in!" emanate from deep within the house, like a fly caught inside the mouth of a Venus flytrap. I open up and see Otis in his crib. Torre is rustling around in his bedroom. The phone rings as I go over to Otis and poke his bellybutton, which is protruding from his jammies. He's got an outie and it looks like a brown tire valve. I hear Torre say "goodbye" to the receiver.

"What time does your flight leave?" I ask.

My boots are wet, dripping on the living room floor.

"6:35! Metro Airport."

"That means we only got 30 minutes!"

"I know, but I'm almost ready," he says.

I get Otis all set for our trip to the airport, which is only ten miles away, but with traffic it seems like 100 miles. I slap on his boots, hat, mittens and coat. I then open up the kitchen drawer, snag Torre's keys and carry Otis outside like a piece of cheap luggage. I buckle him into the child's seat and place a bottle of warm milk in his mouth. Torre eventually flies out of the house like a terrible hurricane, cursing, panting.

We pull up to the terminal and I dodge cabbies, cargo vans, and men with red, bellhop-like costumes. Miraculously, we arrive in enough time, and without killing anyone. I couldn't handle two deaths in one day. The ride over was silent, the tension palpable. As I drove, I looked at Otis in the rearview mirror and attempted to take his mind off of what was happening. I winked at him, bulged my eyes, stuck out my tongue, and made a barrage of goofy noises. Poor kid didn't find it very amusing, though. He's too concerned about his dad. I gave him the nod that says, "Don't worry buddy, your Daddy will be back soon."

I pop the trunk, nab Torre's baggage and set it on the curb while he playfully nuzzles Otis and tells him that he's going away for a few days. Torre doesn't mention the word "mommy," which is smart. Sometimes, that word simply destroys people.

"Give me a call once you get there," I tell him.

"I'm staying at the Vagabond Inn if you need anything."

"Sounds classy."

"It was the only hotel on the strip without a casino inside of it."

"You hire a private dick or anything?"

"Nah, just gonna sniff her out on my own. I've got her phone number from the escort services I found on the net."

We have time, so he grabs one last smoke.

"Torre, what the hell are you gonna do when you get out there?"

"I haven't figured that out yet, George."

"When do you think that will come?"

"As soon as I see her, I'll know," he says, flicking his butt over the hood of his car. "I may see her and leave. I may say 'hello' and see if she wants to get a cup of coffee and talk. I've had that moment play ten million times in my head over the past few months, and I still don't know the right thing to do."

I'm trying to understand. In a way, I do, since I've never met my real parents. I've always felt hollow inside because of that. But since I didn't know them, I never really cared about my parents. The hole in my chest is there, but it's small, the size of a pinhole. Torre, on the other hand, actually loved Candice. He married her. He went on a honeymoon with her. They cuddled in bed when the sheets were cold.

"You never can tell about these things."

"Nope," he says and smiles nervously.

"Call me and let me know when you'll be back."

"Right, like I said, it shouldn't be more than a few days."

I then watch Torre disappear into the oncoming rush of traffic, luggage and cargo.

I don't have anyone to take care of Otis during the day on Saturday, so I call my foster mother and volunteer her for the job. We're not particularly chatty, and she's a bit surprised I've called her for such an emergency. She lives in a trailer park off Wick Road, near the airport. All the neighbors look out their windows as I drive along the gravel road, the nosy bastards.

She answers the door with hair just a bit grayer than I remember. Her body is stout and misshapen and looks like an un-pruned shrub.

"I really appreciate this, Sarah."

"Oh, it's no problem," she says.

I hand Otis over and he plops into her blue-veined hands, her dark scowl hiding as best as it can behind a fake smile. The little guy is wide awake. He's watching everything that's going on around him. For instance, Otis knows this lady was never a good enough mother for me when I grew up. He can tell that although she never hit me or abused me, and that she provided enough food for me as a child, she also never really deserved a Mother's Day card. He sees it all in my discomfort.

"Ohhh, he's a big boy. You're a big boy ain'tcha Otis?"

I avoid eye contact and squirm out of her questions that ensue:

"How are you?"

"How did you get stuck with him?"

"You wanna stay for a cup of coffee before heading to your route?"

"Where'd you say his father went off to?"

I know these cold questions are part of her caring process, but I can't answer without getting deep into it with her. Maybe some day I'll be able to, but not now.

I leave Sarah with a few diapers, some green baby food, some cash. She struggles to hold all these things in her arms. Except for the aging effects, she looks the same: her eyes off in the distant hills, her emotions flubbed like hot grounder to third base.

"I'm late, I gotta run." I turn to leave. "I'll be here after 5:00 to pick him up."

"Ok, we're just gonna watch a little Oprah and do some crossword puzzles. We'll be all right," she says awkwardly.

I have a slight sting in my heart, like maybe I should open up to her and tell her that things were never really that bad. But, I can't, because maybe they were.

"Thanks, Sarah," I say with the sincerity of a caught plagiarist.

Knowing that he's still dead, I walk up to Mr. Johansen's stoop and ring the doorbell anyway. I have his mail and his mailbox is still broken and I still have to deliver it.

For some reason, I expect the old bastard to answer and tell me to stay off his porch. But a young lady answers the door. She's got a notepad, a pen sticking out from behind her locks of dark cherry hair, a ripe smile that bristles the hair on my arm. I'm jarred, rattled, my body murmuring like a symphony warming up before the night's performance.

"Oh. Hello. I didn't really expect anyone to be here." I hand her more useless mail for the deceased Mr. Johansen, the pile of fertilizer.

"Thanks," she says and takes the mail, breathing hard as if working out.

"How did you know Mr. Johansen?"

"He was my grandfather."

"Oh?"

"People say I look more like my grandmother."

Her frame is full and healthy, her cheeks dimpled, flustered. She wears black pants, a black shirt that wraps around her chest and torso.

Her grandmother must have been hot.

"I didn't know him that well, but Mr. Johansen never talked about his family, nor your grandmother." I realize this is the wrong thing to bring up. Maybe that's why Mr. Johansen and I got along so well? Because we're so awkward and crass. "What I mean is that we usually just traded banter and small talk. Snippets of philosophy."

"That was my relationship with him, too." She smiles again and coughs out an embarrassed chuckle. Good toothpaste, this girl. The whitening kind. "He was fine, mentally speaking, until my grandmother died." She gets dejected, almost exhausted. "Then he said he never wanted us kids around. Can you believe that?"

I shrug.

"He said he needed to be alone the last few years of his life," she says. "He was a real bastard."

"Mr. Johansen was a little abrasive, but he was a good guy."

"I guess so." She has forlorn lips, cheeks that pout and droop like heavy sandbags. She kicks the doormat between us.

"What are you doing in there?" I say, breaking her memory.

"Taking inventory while my parents arrange the services."

She's younger than me, though not by much. She's maybe in her early 30's with no wedding ring, no baggage.

"What's Mr. Johansen been hording all these years?"

"Mostly coupons, bottle caps from the 50's. Nothing special."

Sensing that she just wants to be left alone, I back away. "Take it easy in there," I say and point to the old man's lair. "And give my regards to your family."

"Thanks. Hey, wait," she says and hops out on the stoop. "My grandfather's got all this whiskey and vodka in here."

"Is that right?"

"One thing he had in abundance. Would you care for a drink?"

"The way to my heart," I say and step back up to the porch, then look into her lost cucumber eyes. "I would love a drink."

Lucy and I talk throughout the afternoon. We drink cheap vodka and 7up. Staying here means I'll have to hustle to get my route finished and in time to pick up Otis, but it's worth it. Turns out we hit it off and Lucy tells me all about Raymond, Mr. Johansen, her grandfather. How he clamped down like a hermit after her grandmother died and how he didn't do anything but sit and rot and drink. Her parents called and called but he rarely answered the phone, and when he did he was often difficult and pissy.

In turn, I tell her about my foster mother. I tell her about Torre and Otis. I tell her about Candice/Trisha being an escort in Vegas.

"What do you think he'll do?" she says when I mention Torre again, a tinkle of sadness in her words, the glow from the lamp a dark orange-ish sulfur color.

I tell her I don't know and Lucy shifts her body, her lithe chest heaving forward. She suddenly changes her outlook on things, on life. She gets less sad and more realistic with each drink she consumes.

"Your friend Torre sounds a bit psychotic."

"Perhaps," I say.

"Do you think he'd kill her?"

Having never thought of this scenario, I contemplate a moment before I answer. "No," I say. "Rage and anger isn't his thing."

"You never can tell with some men."

I glance at her, see her pain, her scars.

"If he does kill her, it'd be an act of passion," I say, feeling as if I've stolen the line from LA Law. "He doesn't have much motivation."

She doesn't know Torre, so I don't go out of my way to tell her it's a ridiculous idea. It's getting late, so I excuse myself to the bathroom before I get back to the route. After urinating, I check out Mr. Johansen's medication stash. Some Valium. Some Lipitor. Vicodin. Other pills I don't recognize but take anyway.

At the front door we hobble around each other clumsily.

"Good luck with everything." As a last resort, I scratch my name and number on an old Detroit Newspaper. "If you ever need to talk, or if you want to get some coffee or something, give me a call. I know a great place down the street here. Good cappuccino."

"Ok," she says.

I don't necessarily think she's attracted to me, but you never can tell with some women.

At the mouth of the trailer park, I contemplate driving past the entrance to buy some time. I'm not ready for this. But I feel Otis begging me to save him from the boredom of my foster mother, so I turn in rather abruptly, which makes my tires squeal. When I right the car the wheels kick up gravel at the sign of the entrance.

Better than living in a tent! the graffiti on the sign says.

My foster mother answers to door. She's sleepy and un-rested. I feel like shaking some life into her. I want her to be a real person instead of this laggard couch potato. She perks up when she realizes this is not one of the melodramas on HBO, that this is actually the child she supported and took care of for years.

When I get inside the trailer, I feel obligated to stay. She makes coffee and fusspots around the kitchen. Cupboards open up and close. These are the gates to unseen worlds of oatmeal, brown sugar, and lonely cans of tuna fish. The coffee is good. I admit she was always good around the kitchen. I suppose she was meant to be a married housewife all her life instead of a working divorcee with no time for her foster bastard's baseball games. Maybe she's had it rougher than I give her credit for.

We stand and drink coffee in her kitchen. Cream, no sugar.

"Look, Sarah," I say, "I really appreciate you looking after Otis for me. You're the only one I know who wouldn't burn him with a cigarette if he didn't stop crying or accidentally feed him lye for dinner."

She looks ready to crumble and fall to her knees. "Thanks," she whispers.

"Hey. I didn't mean it like that." She never appreciated my sense of humor, which always comes out at the wrong moments. "I'm sorry. That's just a testament to how bad my friends are. Hell, I don't really have many friends except Torre."

"It's still a lousy thing to say."

"I know," I say, shame-sodden. "It's not really the way I intended it to sound."

I take a big gulp and put down the coffee cup. My stomach rumbles as I pick up Otis from the couch. Chocolate mallow mars sit next to him, one of which falls into the crevice of the couch seat and destined to live there forever.

I come back directly to my foster mother in the kitchen, her back facing me. I want her to know how much I love Otis by cuddling him. Rub it in her face a little.

"Thanks again," I say. "This means a lot to me."

With her back still facing me, she sighs like a broken bagpipe.

"I knew I could trust you to help me out."

This isn't a lie. I knew she'd be a reliable person to watch Otis. I put my free hand on her shoulder, which feels like a hot water bag. I try to put all my feeling into this touch from my hand, pushing it deep into her body, burning. I want to make her feel my gratitude, but also my sadness on what I missed out in childhood.

Back at Torre's, there's a message on the answering machine:

"George! Vegas is a shit-hole! True trash. It's got more strip bars than Downriver! Heh heh heh. Well… I found Candice. We met and had drinks at a place called the Mermaid Lounge. She says she's happy out here, though I don't believe her for one fucking minute. The bitch. She's always been a goddamn liar. She's married to some local DJ named Darryl Diamond! Can you believe that? I married a polygamist! Anyway…" he blows static into the receiver. "The next flight out to Detroit is tomorrow at 3:25pm. I haven't made reservations, but hope-fully I'll be on that plane. I'll call with full details tomorrow. I'm gonna go hit the strip while I'm here. Otis buddy, I love you!"

Click.

Before I put him into his crib, Otis and I laze around on the couch and watch old re-runs of Laurel and Hardy and the Three Stooges. I hate both shows because it gets stupid watching the same slapstick for even ten minutes, but those programs also make me feel special, too. It's like I should feel lucky to have them around. Classics have a way of doing that, even though most of them are unbearable to watch.

Friday night in the life of George Rimbaud, U.S. Postal carrier.

In the morning Soul Train is on. Times have changed over the years, but Soul Train sure hasn't. I remember waking up on Saturday mornings to jerk off to Soul Train as a kid. The tight clothes, the short skirts, and every single body part bobbling around like overfilled water balloons. I feel a jump in my pants but decide against it.

How can I masturbate with Otis in the crib over there?

I take some Vicodin from Mr. Johansen's stash and make coffee, a little breakfast. Bored, I pull out Torre's books and thumb through James Baldwin. I love the funny little caricatures in Jaroslav Hasek's "The Good Soldier Svejk." I leave Kerouac on the shelf where it belongs. Otis eventually wakes up and we watch some basketball on NBC.

Torre calls later that morning and says he couldn't find a flight to Detroit Metro, but that he'll be at Detroit City Airport at 7:25pm, which is on the other side of town. The sting of finding out that his wife is married to someone else is obviously inside him. I can hear him feeling ashamed over the phone, like some act of involuntary defecation.

"You ok?" I ask.

"I'm ok. I just didn't know what to expect when I got out here. Now, I don't know what I expect when I get back."

"Well, you have Otis, don't forget that."

"I can never forget that, George," he says. "That's part of the reason I can't forget her."

I have a needy pang in my side as I leave Torre's house. I know exactly where I'm going, and because of this, everything in my chest should feel mangled, unplugged, like a toaster on the fritz. Invading and bold, this move. But, at the same time, barging in on Lucy doesn't feel all that intrusive. It feels natural. I belong on that doorstep.

I park, leave Otis in the car, and knock on Mr. Johansen's door.

Luckily, Lucy peeks her head out the door like a hungry mouse.

"Hi," she says.

"You stayed over last night, eh?" I remember the lilt of her lips when she mentioned she was still undecided about staying the night. She thought it would be odd and twisted.

As she opens the door a little more, I see that Lucy's still in her nightclothes, which reminds me of Otis' pajamas. There are bears with half-opened eyes, pillows and moons. Those bears are sleep-deprived.

"I couldn't fall asleep 'til this 9:00 this morning."

"Lots of work to do?"

"Not much more to go."

"You don't mind me stopping over?" I wave my arms to present my street clothes. "You know, not in uniform and all?"

"No." She rubs the eye crust from her lids. "Not at all. You wanna come in?"

"Just let me grab Otis from the car."

"Ohhh," she squirms. "You brought Otis? I'd love to meet him."

At first, Otis is thrown off by the smell of the old man. He cries for a while, which is unusual. Everything is catching up with him. His mother's a whore. His dad's in Vegas. The crazy mailman is looking after him. A strange, detached lady babysat him. Lucy with her dead grand-father. Tears dribble down Otis' caramel cheeks as he clings to my leg.

"Hey." Lucy crouches and caresses his soft dome. "Don't worry, Otis. Everything is ok." She looks up from Otis and addresses me. "I know how he feels." She looks around the apartment. "This place is a little dingy."

The walls are stained with years of yellow cigarette smoke and other stains of general unhealthiness.

"I suppose it could use a coat of paint," I say. "Of course, you'd have to strip all the carcinogen off the walls first."

She laughs. I do too.

After an awkward pause, I mention picking up Torre at Detroit City Airport later, which is off Conner and Gratiot Avenue, a veritable ghost town in that part of the city.

"That's out where my grandfather is being cremated."

"You mean Gethsemane Cemetery and Crematory?" I ask.

"How did you know?"

"It's a previous route."

"I have to go out tonight to finalize some papers. The crazy bastard bought himself a crypt," she says, sardonic yet amused. "He paid for most of it with his pension. I just have to get out there and give the man a check. Why the hell would you want to be cremated?"

I shrug and picture cigar ashes flowing out of a full ashtray.

"What time do you have to be there?"

"I told the guy around 6:00."

"You need a ride? We're picking Torre up at 7:00."

She hesitates, foresees the awkwardness she's getting into.

"Sure," she says and smiles and I think perhaps the endeavor is harmless after all. Maybe a platonic adventure with the mailman is exactly what she needs to forget about her grandfather. "Besides, I'm in no condition to drive."

"What do you mean?"

"I found my grandfather's stash of pain pills last night."

"Pain pills?" I say.

We hop on I-94, head east, and then curl past Hamtramck once we get on I-75. We exit on Conner and we bear witness to the bare trees, abandoned buildings and barren streets. These are the broken bones of a once-proud city, too old to be mended back to health.

A man in a stiff opal suit greets us as we pass through the glass doors of the front office. The man's hair is badly cut and his body is lop-sided like a dilapidated tree house. You can tell the man preys on the dead. You can tell God made him specifically for this job, and only he and God know this (and me).

Otis and I hang back as Lucy and the man walk into his office and conduct business. I look outside at the bone marrow-colored night descending upon Detroit. As it starts to rain clumps of sleet, I think about having funeral parlor sex with Lucy. Then I hear the soft whispers of the dead bouncing off the marble floors and walls, telling me to knock it off.

I don't exactly know what I want from Lucy. Perhaps nothing but this day. Perhaps more than companionship. Perhaps a person to help me make my life more difficult, more worthwhile.

Lucy eventually emerges from the man's office. She looks annoyed, exasperated, as if a bank teller told her she had no money left.

"You ok?" I ask.

"He was so business about everything," she whispers. "He didn't smile or console me or anything. Just asked for the check and he had a poker face the whole time."

"He's been doing this for decades, you can't blame him."

"The mother fucker didn't even talk about the weather! Like my grandfather didn't matter!"

"Lucy, you can be certain your grandfather matters to him," I say and touch her forearm to console her.

I then hoist Otis up onto my hip. On the way out, I turn around to nod to the man, a look that says 'I know who you are, and I will never forget you.' I'm also proud I didn't tell Lucy that her grandfather only matters in this man's ledger at the end of the month.

Detroit City Airport is mainly used for corporate and private aircraft, but there are occasional commercial flights. The place is small and clogged with uncaring receptionists and soda machines that are out of order. There's a lounge with a bartender that looks like he's about to lose his grip. Maybe because he resembles Isaac from the Love Boat.

I order two beers and a juice with a maraschino cherry for Otis.

"So what did Torre do out there in Sin City?" Lucy takes a sip from the fuzzy head of beer.

"He met Candice at a bar and talked to her."

"And?"

"That's it. She's staying in Vegas. She married another man."

"How could she do something like that?"

"What? Abandon Otis and her husband to strip and whore around in Vegas?"

"Yeah, what the hell?"

"Things are always more complicated than they seem, I suppose."

"I guess," she says with a bothersome look on her face. "Why don't you seem to care? Doesn't this affect you?"

I look into Lucy's eyes and see the Arctic Circle in them. But maybe not that far. Maybe I see northern Canada. Saskatchewan.

"What makes you think I don't care?"

"I don't know. This thing with your foster mother. This thing with Torre. Even with my grandfather's death. You just seem to take things as they are."

"Is there any other way?"

"There are tons of different ways," she says.

This tone is more condescending than I care to admit.

"I know. But you do by what you're taught."

"I still think what Candice did was shitty."

"Me too. I feel bad. I'm just saying there's probably a reason. And there's things we cannot understand in this life. Maybe it's not for us to understand?"

She stays silent for a minute and considers my aloofness. Then her eyes connect to mine and I'm trapped. "You're a good friend, George.

You know that?" This sudden shift to compassion confuses me and makes my stomach drop into the gutter. Her lips are glossy and I want to kiss her. This feeling hurts.

"Thanks."

"You're good with kids, too. Otis really likes you."

"Otis and I get along great."

"Thanks again for taking me to the crematory," she says sweetly.

I fawn a bit. "I didn't realize how sexy a sentence like that could actually be," I say.

She laughs again and so do I.

Torre eventually emerges from the ramp, an accordion that connects to the terminal, stoned and disheveled. Wearily, he takes Otis from my arms and kisses him gently, quietly.

"You been waiting long?" Torre's lips clasp together in dryness.

"Not too long." I step aside so he can see that Lucy is with me. "This is Lucy," I say. "Her grandfather just died. I took her over to Gethsemane Cemetery. He's being cremated."

"Nice to meet you." Torre shakes her hand. "Sorry about your grandfather."

"Sorry to hear about your situation as well," Lucy says.

Torre looks at me and I shrug, then look away, embarrassed. I know I shouldn't have spilled the beans, but I think he understands my ploy to score with Lucy by evoking empathy and exposing his situation.

"It's nothing, really." Torre looks Otis in his big brown eyes. "We're better off. Right buddy? This way, everything is finalized."

I get back onto I-94 and head west toward signs that say Chicago. Perhaps we could all move to Chicago, I think, and function as some ham-fisted family. We'd be connected by being disconnected from the ones that we should love, but don't.

I drop off Torre and Otis first, which is an old move, but it gives me extra one-on-one time to talk to Lucy before I drop her off at her grandfather's.

As we exit the car, Torre looks relieved, but tired and hungry.

"You guys want to come in for a beer?" he says.

"No thanks," Lucy says. "We don't want to impose."

"Wash the Vegas out of your hair, Torre, and get some rest."

"It was nice to meet you Lucy," Torre says.

We part after I help him carry the luggage in.

With Otis on his hip he says, "Thanks a lot, man. You don't know how much I really appreciate this."

"No problem," I say and nod my head back at the car. "You got any advice here?"

"I married an evasive stripper, George. I'm a single parent of a child that's not even mine. I'm about as drunk as can be right now. I'm not sure my advice is going to help."

"Still."

"Just be yourself," he says.

I touch Otis' nose, nod to Torre and walk off the porch.

Lucy and I hit Fort Street and head to her grandfather's house. I turn onto Polk Street and see all the familiar mail boxes. I breathe in the ten second glimpses to their complicated lives: Mrs. Diaz with her diabetes; the Fitzpatrick family, whose son recently ran away from home because he beat up the principal of Melvindale High School; Mr. Mahoney and his lifetime subscription to Car and Driver, the constant clots of grease underneath his fingernails, a re-built Pontiac Firebird inside his garage, which never seems to get fully re-built. These people get bills and foreclosure letters and birthday cards and useless fashion fillers that clutter up their mailboxes, yet they continue to live their lives.

"Here we are," I say and shift into park, the car's engine idling, the muffler coughing into Mr. Johansen's driveway.

Lucy lingers while she retrieves the keys from her purse.

"You want to come in?"

"I do," I say. "But I can't. I have some things to do."

She harrumphs. "It's just as well. I have to get back to my parents tonight and tell them that, aside from the stack of useless coupons and delicious pain pills, my grandfather had absolutely nothing of value."

"He most certainly had some things of value," I say. "He just didn't know how to treat them."

She smiles, leans in, and kisses my cheek. The smell of her perfume sweeps by, the scent of her face soon thereafter. It's an earthy smell, like a shallow, muddy pond.

"Bye, George."

Lucy withdraws from the car, the sod-like scent lingering. I watch her walk up the steps. Lucy then turns around and waves from the porch, her face a soft pillow, her body a warm blanket I'd like to drape myself with, her mind a drug I'd like to consume. She then slams the door shut, hard and cold, exactly the way Mr. Johansen would have done it.

I back the car out of the driveway and set sights for my foster mother's trailer in Taylor. There's something I have to talk to her about. Something that'll probably make both of our lives more difficult, but certainly more worthwhile.

MT. TRASHMORE

When the weather gets warm, odd things poke up from the landfill ground and pose hazards to the skiers: metal fence posts, car fenders, work desks, old clunky typewriters. We find this stuff and rip it out because we're the Riverview Highlands maintenance crew and this is our duty. Most of us take this job seriously.

This morning, before anyone takes the slope, I punch in and see the sun shining across the snow, like there's a film of plastic-wrap on top of the mountain, a tarp of translucent skin. I grab a cup of decaf and notice something like a leg sticking out of the ground near the back moguls of The Cyclone Run.

This, invariably, is the beginning of my day.

I yell to Benny in the back office, "I'm going out!" He just grunts while I scamper away. As we've come to realize, these objects—these discarded storm doors or slightly used pipefittings jutting out from the snow—could be anything, really. Which is exciting.

I keep the object in sight and head out on my 600HO Fusion Polaris snowmobile, standard issue for all the grounds crew at Riverview Highlands. In summer we use ATVs. I get close enough to see that it is indeed a leg, perhaps made of titanium alloy, or some other indestructible metal.

From a few feet away, I see the leg has a rubber foot attached and life-like toes. It must have once belonged to a woman. The nails are painted a deep burgundy, almost chocolate; the arch is dainty and delicate. It's quite attractive.

With all my might, I tug on the metal calf of the leg, but she doesn't budge. She's stuck in there good. Adrenaline burning in my throat, I blaze back to the office, the spring wind blowing in my face. The wind is fresh, feels good. Tears seep out of the corners of my eyes.

"Hey, Benny." I re-enter the office, my glasses fogging up from the warmth.

Benny grunts again and I watch him pace throughout the office like there's a riot outside. I check the space heater near the window. It's a fire hazard, breathes orange heat near a desk full of papers. One false move and we'd be toasting marshmallows.

"You see that leg out there?" I take off my glasses and can hardly see the mountain in the background. It's just a bright, fuzzy blur tightening my eyes.

"You know the drill, Touhy." Benny never looks up from his clipboard. I put my glasses back on and see Benny's lips look bruised, purple, and he's got bed-head, but it's not style, just a lack of sleep and time.

Benny's the foreman of our maintenance crew. I've been sleeping with his younger sister, Rhonda, for the past two years. Rhonda's thin as a rail with long hammertoes and flat fingers, really flat fingers. The docs say she's terminal, some fickle cancer in her marrow that won't go away. Oftentimes, I imagine blanched bones drying in a desert, tumbleweeds. Rhonda and I keep our affair quiet from most people. Her brother included.

Benny looks at me with his soggy face. Some say he's special in that extra chromosome way. Me, I think he looks like a mudfish with segmented eyes, a bottom-dweller from the depths of Lake Superior.

"Benny, you gotta see this thing. It's a chick's leg!"

Benny isn't usually interested in artificial limbs, or anything else we drudge up from the ground. He's been at Riverview Highlands, or Mt. Trashmore, as we like to say, for over ten years now, and he's seen it all.

When I first interviewed for the job, he told me all about the non-biodegradable dreck that'd pop up from the landfill during the spring. Twenty years ago, the city of Riverview heaped acres of dirt onto a pile of garbage and called it a ski slope, then had the audacity to charge twenty bucks per head, even more for rentals. I remember Benny telling me he wouldn't be surprised if he saw a pocket watch with Jimmy Hoffa's inscription on it someday.

That would be something.

"Do me a favor and take it out. Without all the rigmarole."

"Ok. Ok. Don't get 'em into a knot."

"Then get up to The Bunny Run. The chairlift is on the fritz again." With the back of his knuckle, Benny rubs one of his large, bulbous eyes. He's always high on stress. "Probably the motor belts. Ron and Butter are up there already."

I noodle for a minute.

"Go see if they need help, Touhy."

"You sure you don't want to see this thing? I mean, it's a chick's leg." I act like this explanation should explain it all. "Little toes are painted and everything."

"Touhy!"

"What? It's cute."

"Get out there! Now!" Benny points to the door with his ball-point, clicks the end three times like Morse code. "Before the skiers see this fucking leg or whatever it is."

I salute like a soldier and say, "Yes, sir!"

I take it in stride. Benny only yells when he's serious. We try to keep it aloof, but sometimes he acts like he's my older brother. Benny looks out for me—solid raises each year, looks the other way when I need a day off, buys me lunch when I'm broke—and I appreciate that. He's a mentor in some dysfunctional way.

I hump out to the tool shed. Grabbing a clamp and a heavy chain, I pack 'em up on my Polaris and take off again for the leg, the wind pushing my face, whistling into my nostrils. The wind burns, but it's a good kind of burn.

I situate the clamp on the girl's leg, hook the chain up to the back of my snowmobile and tug the thing out. Ploop! The spring sun has done its part, so with the strength of the snowmobile, the leg dislodges from the softened ground rather easily. It's like pulling a popsicle out of its wrapping.

I drag the leg along the snow and hit the brakes. Momentum carries the leg toward the back of my snowmobile, the metal skidding along the ice and it eventually comes to a complete stop. I cut the engine and everything goes quiet.

At first, I'm disappointed. It's simply a device that replaces a leg below the knee. I half expected the rest of an entire woman to follow, that maybe an alloy skeleton—like some female Terminator from a futuristic war—was buried in the ground. That maybe she was waiting for someone like me to save her, that maybe together we could rescue the new world from destruction, chaos. Alter the past for a better future.

My initial disappointment dissolves when I pick the leg up and hold it in my hands. It's heavy, covered with earthy sod. I like it. It feels important. Like maybe it was the first artificial leg ever invented. I think of all the different women who could've possessed this leg. Amputees. Birth defects. I think about how hard high school must've been for this person. Wives from Chernobyl, daughters from Three Mile Island. I think of a woman intrigued with new technology, tossing away the leg for one made of carbon fiber, hoping her new limb would bring luck, joy.

I also think of my mother. She isn't missing a leg, not that I know of, but she's been gone from our lives for some time now. I think of her smooth calf. I think of her toes at the beach, embedded into the sand. For years after she left, my father refused to put up pictures of her in the house. Now, out of the blue, he keeps one near his bedside table.

With leg in hand, I check the hole in the ground. It's dark and looks like a gopher's hole. I shove my bare hand inside, the dirt lodging underneath my fingernails. It feels like someone might grab my wrist and yank me inside the landfill.

But I'm not so lucky.

I stand up and look at the office in the distance, the shining red bulb at the top of the communications tower, blinking on and off. The Detroit skyline is in the distance, the Ambassador Bridge swallowed up by smog from Zug Island.

I look at the leg again and feel a deep pull in my stomach. Underneath clumps of dirt and grass, the metal is shiny and still perfect. There's no rust whatsoever. I clean the leg as best as I can and place it, delicately, into my canvas bag, the zippered teeth gnashing shut.

Approaching The Bunny Run, I see Butter up on the main tower with the circuit box open, the red and green and black wires hanging out of the metal box like intestines flailing out from an open gut wound. The trams are dead-still, empty. They're usually in motion by this time of the day, wobbling up and down the mountain, ready to be sat on by skiers.

Ron is on the ground with a walkie-talkie close to his mouth, breath blooming out in white puffs. Off in the distance, you can hear one of the artificial snow makers kicking to life with a weak whir. They're on timers, and I imagine an old man getting out of bed, suppressing a coughing fit, shutting off the alarm clock with a slow, beaten hand.

"You guys see the leg this morning?"

Ron is looking up at Butter, his face and neck unshaven, the hair a rusty sulfur color. We're both looking up at Butter now.

"Didn't see no leg, Simon," Ron says with a calm southern drawl, then, in the same breath, shouts up at Butter, "You almost done up there? What's taking so long?"

From twenty feet above, I watch Butter as he pinches the smoke dangling from his chubby lips, drags a deep drag, and then drops the lit cigarette down toward the both of us, as if to say, "I'll be done when I'm done, Fuckos!"

The red bud falls like a dying star and hits the snowy ground with a sizzle. The end of the cigarette is suddenly a soggy mixture of ash and tobacco, blackened soot.

Ron looks at the butt, then up at Butter. "You gotta be careful with that shit!"

Butter flips us the bird.

I chuckle even though Ron is totally right.

Since Trashmore's opened, there've been only a few explosions; a fatal one in 1984, and three minors in the past seven years. There are NO SMOKING signs all over the mountain, but the skiers often get the itch to smoke and, unexpectedly, of course, light up near an open pocket of gas and BOOM! They get blown back twenty or so feet. The injuries never amount to much—herniated discs, groin pulls, banged-up tailbones—but with an unstable landfill like this, you never know.

Me, I don't smoke.

"Son of a bitch." Ron rubs his wet nose, the glassy snot running into his moustache. By mid-day, his upper lip will be salty with this mucous, his lips chapped from the licking.

The trams then magically kick to life. Butter closes the lid of the circuit box and lets out a happy burp, for his job is done for the day. He'll spend the next few hours up in the maintenance shack on the other side of Toboggan Hill reading Penthouse Forums and eating black licorice.

Ron and I watch Butter's descent; his bare hands clutching each peg of the tower, his knuckles white and knobby.

"He's lucky he's so good with this electrical shit."

Ron's good at giving guff to Butter. To everyone, really.

"Yeah." I kick snow over the cigarette, a discreet burial that only I partake in. "It's the only thing he knows how to do. You ever see his house? It's a fucking pig sty."

"I hope he falls and breaks his ass."

"Me too." I laugh. "But who'd fix the trams?"

Ron takes his gaze off Butter, places it onto me, his milky blue eyes awash in suspicion, maybe even hurt.

"What?" I say.

"You know damn well 'what,'" he says and looks back up.

It's only then do I realize Ron is next in line for Butter's position. It'd be a nice pay hike for Ron, not to mention eliminating the disgrace of playing second fiddle.

Butter's top gun of our maintenance crew, and he'll retire soon. He's only 49, but he's been working for the city of Riverview since twenty. Just about the same age when I started. I was twenty-one when they hired me to groove the snow and salt the walkways. I had high hopes back then. I thought I'd learn more about snow making technology to open a ski resort of my own. King of the Hill, I'd call it.

Butter eventually plants his feet on the snow and says, "Piece of cake." He then unhooks his harness to let his belly sag back to its natural position, the metal belts clanking at his sides.

They never let me do jobs like this because I get vertigo. Not that I can't fix the problems. I take engineering courses over at U of M Dearborn. I've been there for six years now. But everybody at the slope says I'm unqualified, that I lack "real world" experience.

Butter gets a serious squinch to his face. "You found a leg, Simon?" he asks.

I look up at the top of the tower, amazed he could hear me from so far up. I thought that hairy jungle at the beginning of his ear canal would clog just about any sound.

"You guys wanna see it? It's a woman's leg."

"Not really." Butter then spits a goober into the snow.

"Don't take that leg off grounds," Ron says. "You know the rules."

The rules are we're not allowed to take anything from the landfill home, even though Butter does it all the time. He lives in Hamtramck, which is a Polish section of Detroit, and his house is filled with all sorts of miscellaneous electrical gadgets from Trashmore: unused connectors, relays, strips of wire, cogs, sprigs, whatever he can smuggle away in his pocket or fanny pack.

Ron radios Benny at home base and says, "Trams are a go!" and we all head our separate ways. I head back to the office, and as I do, I see the first skier at the bottom of the hill. It's a middle-aged man wrestling around with his rentals like it's his first time.

At home, I sneak the leg inside my room, though I know it's not an ideal spot. The best place would be the garage, out next to the the lawnmower, out with the stink of grass and gasoline, next to the weed-whacker and the spider's nests.

It's Friday, and although my father isn't yet home from the bowling alley, he soon will be, the golden sway of Miller High Life's making him light-headed and talkative.

My father doesn't drink as much as he used to, which is a good thing. The lack of suds keeps his belly from bloating. Nowadays, his drug is sleep. It's hard to imagine a former Navy officer getting addicted to sleep of all things, but he just can't seem to get enough.

Since my mother left, he's all but abandoned the vestiges of a dedicated seaman. He doesn't make his bed in the morning, he doesn't do his pushups, doesn't keep his footlocker clean, he doesn't even get that glint in his eyes when he sees a freighter chugging through the Detroit River. His slovenly life has finally taken over the entire house. You should see the basement. It's a spread of dirty clothes and junk piled upon junk. I call this morass the Sea of Madness.

When he's had a few pops, my father talks baseball. The old man played college ball for a small Division II school in Ohio. During his junior year, he took some rusted spikes to the foot turning a double play. A nasty, almost gangrene infection ensued and he missed the entire season, ending his career.

"That's baseball," he'd told me.

I guess he later joined the Navy to prove he was still a man.

I, too, had college baseball aspirations. I was an all-state catcher in high school. But that was around the time my mother went back to Thailand, and after she left I suddenly lost the taste for leather gloves, the tang of dip, the ping of aluminum bats.

We're both not really sure why my mother left. We're only sure of the fact that she did leave. It's like the answer you find in the answer key in the back of the workbook but are too lazy to figure out the equation later on. My father came up to me after batting practice one day, took the gear bag out of my grasp, and said, "Your mother's left us, Simon."

With the way they had been ignoring each other, not even bothering to fight anymore, I should've expected it.

There was an uneasy look in my father's eyes, extra weight in his distended belly. He had a bad haircut at the time, way too boxy for his droopy face. Afterwards, we went to a Coney Island to get gyros slathered with Tzatziki dressing, my steel cleats clacking along the cement as we walked to the parking lot and toward his Caprice Classic.

That was that. We simply started life anew. We didn't cling to the backs of milk cartons or paste "lost" posters or hire a private dick. My father didn't even try to stop her, just stepped aside and let her walk out the front door, suitcase in hand. We don't get postcards or letters or collect phone calls from unknown payphones in the middle of Thailand.

Of course, the old man knows more about the "why" than I do. When pressed—like the time my mother's dentist called to set up a cleaning appointment—he tells people that she went back to her native land to find her real parents, that she was adopted.

Everybody knew that. She had white parents, after all.

"Only thing your mother left behind," he said as we folded our pitas and brought them up to our mouths, the chunky, white sauce dripping on the wax paper, "was her brown skin and slanted eyes."

These traits, however, are so watered down they're hardly noticeable. Some people, like the guys at work for example, will occasionally call me gook or chink, just to razz me, and I think it's kind of funny in a way. Like when I come up unnoticed, Butter always says, "Charlie in the bushes! Where the hell did you come from?"

But it's not like my mother had the "me so horny" accent.

People often assume my father was stationed in China, that he had his pick among that year's crop of fine, pre-pubescent virgins. Like he slapped down the dowry, slung my mother over his shoulder and hopped the first boat back the America.

Both my parents grew up here in Michigan.

I place the bag on my bed and look out my bedroom window. The days are getting longer. Pink clouds settle into the sky, easing themselves onto the sun. I imagine it's like lowering your bottom half into a hot bath. If I weren't so eager to get at this leg, I might be the kind of person who would sit and enjoy such things a little longer.

But I'm not that kind of person.

I open the bag and my heart constricts. I love the leg already. I pull it out and twist it and bend it into different positions, straighten it, stroke it, needle it, compare it to own my leg. I like how the metal stays cold, even after playing with the leg for so long.

"Foot fetish." I say this to myself. After an hour of admiring, that's the only thing I can really think about, that I'm now a foot fetish-ist, which doesn't feel bad, though it doesn't seem like my sort of thing. I can, however, live with the parameters of the fetish. I can live with the label. I've lived with labels all my life.

We've fallen into a comfortable routine.

I've named the leg Madison, and every night I race home after work and set up our nook in the garage, our cozy fortress of love. Madison and I watch movies. Listen to the radio. Read a quiet book. Play house. We watch old science fiction flicks: *Plan 9 From Outer Space*, *When Worlds Collide*, *Forbidden Planet*.

On special nights, I give Madison a bath in mineral spirits and paint her toenails. I like the colors the nail polish companies have invented: French Kiss, Strawberry Daiquiri, Tempest, Champagne, Rosehip, Tiramisu. They're delicious. Some even glow and change colors in the light. There are odorless and non-toxic kinds, too. But I like the toxins. I like the smell.

At the end of every evening, I pile up some blankets and lay Madison to sleep on Roger's old bed. We buried Roger behind the garage last fall, so he won't mind. He'd just be glad his bed isn't going to waste.

The vet never did explain to us how a cat contracts the AIDS virus—whether it was unprotected sex or tainted fish skins from the garbage or sharing intravenous needles, we'll never know—but Roger had it, and that was that. My father dug the hole after I found him behind the couch, the fur shedding his body, his skin cold and clammy like refrigerated lunchmeat.

I gave the eulogy.

Rhonda, I'm afraid, has become suspicious. I haven't seen her in a week, which is rare. She's taken to leaving covert messages on our machine lately. After the first few go unanswered, I notice frustration slipping into her voice, the low timbre elevated to a tinny shrill.

"Johnny Boy? This is Hannah O'Meara. The eggs are in the basket. Mama bird is keeping them warm. Call me back with further instructions. *Today.*"

Rhonda and I are so accustomed to secret meetings that we've kept up the façade. On our first date, we snuck out to the roller rink and pretended Benny wasn't my boss. We ate onion rings and kissed underneath the maple trees in her front yard. Later that night, she crept back into her house in through the backdoor, shoes off, slinking down the dark hallway like a burglar, her hands sliding against the walls to keep her balance. No one suspected a thing.

The thrill of getting together under false pretenses was exciting. For weeks I'd slip away from the dinner table and tell my father lies. Blatant, stupid, like I wanted to get caught.

"Goin' to the movies, Pop!"

I'd be at the door with flowers, maybe a teddy bear.

"With who?"

"Uh. Steve."

"You don't know any Steve! And who are those flowers for?"

I'd pretend I was a desperate husband having an affair with another married lady. I'd ditch my imaginary family, stick my imaginary wife with the imaginary laundry and the imaginary marital aids. In my fantasy, my wife had stopped having sex with me long ago.

A year after our first date, Rhonda got the bad news. She stopped going to college and spent more time at home wrapped in blankets and worry. Meetings after her chemotherapy were the worst. She always had that gaunt, jaundiced look to her face, like someone had dusted her mouth and eyes with a puff of uranium flakes.

After the diagnosis, she began confronting me. "If you ever break up with me, Simon, just be honest." We'd often swing on the swings behind the abandoned elementary school. Rhonda needed fresh air after the poison. She liked to feel her stomach drop out from underneath her. Swinging cleansed her. "If it's because I'm dying, I can handle it."

She always talked about breaking up after each chemo session. Like she sensed her inevitable death and wanted to experience the break-up before she actually died, which made sense in a way.

"I'd never break up with you because you're dying, Rhonda."

We'd swing in silence.

"I don't want you to stay out of pity, either."

To that I'd usually have no answer. I'd give her a shrug, maybe scoff, and then I'd try to get higher than her on the swings, always higher.

When Rhonda got tired, we'd sneak back to my place and I'd put my mother's old afghan over her curled-up body. She would sleep the rest of the afternoon. I'd set a glass of chocolate milk on the bedside table, maybe a glass of chlorinated tap. I'd watch her and think about how this person might not be here one day.

Now, I listen to another message on the machine:

"This is the phone company," she says. "We believe your wires are crossed. We need to investigate further. Please call us at your convenience."

It's only then do I realize the messages are a silly game. From her uninspired voice, I think Rhonda realizes it, too.

On Tuesday, after I get home from work, Rhonda shows up at my doorstep, a surprise visit. She's pounding at the door before I get a chance to peel off my work clothes. I scurry down the hall and look out the front window. She's standing there stamping her feet, the slush jumping up and cascading back down onto the welcome mat. She must've been waiting for me around the block, prowling.

I open up the storm door and act like nothing is wrong. "Hey Rhonda," I say. "How's tricks?"

The weather's getting milder, but Rhonda's bundled up in a puffy goose down jacket, a wool scarf rubbing against her skin and irritating her entire collar area, wisps of brown hair trailing out of her winter cap. She looks sicker than usual.

"Hey Simon." Her voice is scratchy today, like she's been eating glass, or smoking cigars. I avoid her eyes and focus on her cheeks, which remind me of the "Bordeaux" color I just painted on Madison's toes the other day. She must have been outside for a while.

"I need to talk to you."

Before I offer to take her coat, my dad lets out a fizzled snore from his Barca lounger in the family room. He then jams his hand into his underpants and has a good scratch. That's his trademark. Next, he'll be whiffing those fingers.

Before that happens, I say, "Maybe we should go out in the backyard and talk?"

"Fine by me. What about my shoes?"

I notice an edge to her voice, irritation, like there's a boil on the back of her neck that she can't get to. "Leave 'em on," I say.

We walk through the kitchen and I pick up a fake apple from the wicker chicken on the table, gripping it like a baseball, forking it, knuckling it, and then palming it like a change-up. It'll help me think.

Help me feel in control.

Rhonda's shoes slosh and squeak when she hits the linoleum in the kitchen. We exit out the back and I close the sliding glass door behind us.

"What's up?"

I quickly take in the backyard: the birdbath in the corner filled with shitty water, two bald whitewalls sitting along the chain-link fence. There's also a lawn jockey. His clothes are discolored from the harsh weather and his face has a frozen stare.

This lawn jockey will be the only one watching our demise.

Rhonda gives me that look and says, "You know, I haven't seen you in like a week, Simon."

Suddenly, I'm tired, and there's a needy pang in my heart. My goals, lately, have become shortsighted. My only goal now is to get Rhonda out of the backyard and on her way home as fast as I can. I've stopped going to school at nights to have more time with Madison. I've even considered moving out to my own apartment for more privacy.

"Stop exaggerating." I wave her off. "It's been a few days at most."

Her brown eyes turn black and hard like coal and then I imagine Rhonda sitting at home near the telephone each night, gripping the cord, waiting for the damned thing to ring. Next to her orange-colored meds, I imagine a can of Vernors on the night table, her fuzzy skunk slippers at the foot of the bed. Rhonda loves skunks. She says that if you remove their stink glands they can be great as household pets.

I see the worry in her face, deep in her brows, which burns me up. She doesn't need to worry about me. She only need to worry about herself. It's this unselfishness that bothers me most.

"Rhonda, what can I say?"

I sigh like a soap opera character and look into the sky, which is pink, like the flesh of uncooked chicken. Must be nearing six o'clock, and for a moment, I listen to the television inside the house. The murmurings of Wheel of Fortune. I can hear the studio audience clapping, consonants yelled out in haste, the tick of the wheel. I can see my father slumped in the armchair, chest heaving, graham cracker crumbs in his lap.

"I miss you, Simon. That's all."

I don't answer. Instead, I imagine Vanna White turning over letters, a sequined dress hugging her thickened and mid-aged caboose. She's walking across the stage toward the end of the puzzle, but she's limping for some reason.

I look closer and see that Vanna has a prosthetic leg.

"I've just been busy."

"Can we hang out tonight?"

"I can't. I got homework. Plus there's a Tiger game on tonight. Grapefruit League. They're televising from Lakeland."

It's a lame excuse. Normally, I'd sneak Rhonda into my room and we'd watch the sunny Florida sun on the television screen. She'd help me with my homework and we'd eat Hydrox sandwich crèmes and she'd hide underneath the covers when my dad would get up to use the bathroom down the hall, passing gas with each lumbering step. Rhonda always laughed a bit too loud whenever that happened, always attempting to unravel our secret.

"Well, ok." She says this with a dead tinkle, her lips slack and floppy. My stomach binds at the thought of racing into the garage to be with Madison.

Rhonda then heads past me, not looking me in the eye.

"Wait." I walk toward the gate with my hand on the shoulder of her goose down. Like how I think a gentlemen might act, I open up the gate, the metal pole cold to the touch, and we give each other a noncommittal peck. Her nose is wet like a dog's.

"See you soon, I guess?"

"Yeah. Definitely soon, Rhonda."

The words sound like a lie because they are.

Rhonda walks down the sidewalk from the top of our driveway, and while she does, I realize that she doesn't have a prosthetic leg. Underneath her brown corduroys are just regular legs, which are attractive, too, if you were into that sort of stuff.

Few days later, I'm out in the garage when I hear my father break open the sliding glass door and enter the backyard. I jump up and hide Madison underneath Roger's old blankets. Grabbing a nearby magazine, I watch a swatch of old tabby fur floating up from the blanket. The hunk of fur stays suspended in the filtered sunlight for a moment.

Then the garage door roars open and I feel the spring air rush in, motor oil and dust making its escape. My father is standing there in his yard work clothes, too much denim for one man, smiling but silent. There are grass stains on his jeans, paint stippling on his Lions sweatshirt. I haven't seen these clothes in years.

"Thought I'd find you out here."

"Just reading," I say, holding up the evidence.

"Sure." He walks in, ignoring me. There's something bright about his face as he picks up his brown gardening gloves, slides them over his swollen, puffy hands. I notice that he's finally removed his wedding band.

The day outside is brilliant, warmest to date.

"What're you up to, Dad?"

"Well, I thought I'd get some fertilizer on this lawn."

I look over at the dead sod. It's soggy and damp from the recently melted snow and, beyond that, hasn't been cared for in years. My father was once a proud lawnmower, a connoisseur of pest and weed control, irrigation systems.

"Little early to put fertilizer on the lawn, isn't it?"

Dad rips a bag open, the nitrogen dust unfurling.

"Forgot to do this last fall."

"Last fall?"

"Yeah, I didn't do this last fall." He grunts, rising from his squat. "What's the big deal?"

"Forgive me if I seem confused."

He wheels the rotary spreader over to the open bag and says, "What's that supposed to mean?"

"Never mind," I say and flip through my magazine, *Beyond Amputation*. Nothing registers, not the stories about rehabilitation or adjusting to life without limbs or the Vietnam war stories, not even the glossies of prosthetic arms or metal hands and hooks.

My father is usually sleeping in his chair around this time, defeated. With another grunt, he dumps the bag into the spreader, stands straight, and puts his hands on his hips. For a fleeting moment, he stares at the oil stains on the foundation of the garage. This is where my mother's car sat for years after she left. We sold it for scrap last summer. One stain looks like a pterodactyl, another like an empty cape.

I would like to believe both my father and I are thinking about where she is at this exact moment: maybe asleep on a bamboo mat, breathing in the fragrance of the nearby rice paddies, the seasonal rain pelting a soft white dress, rickshaws scrambling down the streets like insects. On the flipside, I hope she has the heart to think about her son and husband once in a while: how we miss her cooking, how the laundry continually goes undone, how we beg for the warmth of her mouth, the stubbly nook of her underarm.

"You should get out," my father tells me. "You've been spending way too much time in this filthy garage."

"Look who's talking!"

My father points at me and yanks his thumb back toward the outside, as if telling me nothing will break his mood. Trying to ignore him, I listen as he wheels the spreader out to the lawn, whistling zip-a-dee-doo-da, starting his famous crisscross pattern, the one that earned him Best Lawn back in 1995.

The ski slopes are now closed for the season and we're officially in Spring clean-up mode.

More and more objects emerge from the ground: needles, stethoscopes, bags of blood and fat that look like strawberry-vanilla shakes. The last load the city of Riverview buried in this landfill must have been a heap of hospital supplies. It's nasty, and the extra hours to clean it up keeps me from Madison.

One thing is a fact: Throw it away and if the material doesn't degrade naturally, it'll resurface someday. That's just the way it is.

On Friday, the Environmental Protection Agency shows up for their annual spring inspection. The inspectors—all of them men—spread out around the Highlands and nod to us solemnly, test equipment in their hands, poking the ground, and checking for methane output. This inspection always puts Benny in a bad mood, and I'm not sure why.

"How you guys doin'?" I say to one of the fellows, a portly, sour-looking chap with dry skin. He ignores me like I'm the runt of the litter.

Every year I try to be nice to the inspectors. They seem like a very official and dedicated organization. They wear blue windbreakers with large yellow block letters on the back that say "EPA." Each jacket also has a name stitched in cursive on front near the breast: Ronald. Bret. Allen. Nick "the Dick."

I only wish I had a windbreaker like that.

Hours pass by, and as I'm out hauling a bundle of debris to the Dumpster, Ron buzzes up on his 4-wheeler and says, "Benny wants us all in the break room."

I straighten my back and feel a pinch in the nether region.

"What does he want?"

"Bastards want to shut us down."

"Who?" I take off my gloves. "EPA?"

"Yup. The Dark Side."

"After all these years?"

Ron fingers his moustache because he's the kind of guy to actually have a moustache. He looks like he's on the verge of puking as he says, "Break room, Simon. Pronto." With that, he salutes and hums away, the wheels kicking up flecks of mud.

I dump the debris and head on over.

The smell of old pizza and PBJ hits me hard when I enter the break room, a small windowless cell that has all the amenities of any other break room in the workforce: microwave, plastic sporks, relish packets, a flag of gnats hovering above the garbage can. This fustiness is a staple, a legend.

Everybody is here: Benny, Ron, Butter, Mandy and Sandy—the Pelican Sisters. They run the registers at the Pro Shop and look exactly like pelicans. I sit with a cup of hot cocoa and wait for Benny to address us. He's up front with that clipboard, clicking his pen.

Benny then clears his throat and says, "As you may or may not be aware, EPA and the City have decided to shut down Riverview Highlands as a ski resort." He pauses to gather his seriousness. "The golf course will remain open, but the extra maintenance associated with the landfill has become way too problematic."

There are groans. Mostly from Butter, who has indigestion, I think. He's always popping those chalky tablets into his mouth. He chomps them wildly while his jowls flap around like Dizzy Gillespie, except that Butter's white and musically inept and has an ulcer. With his chair propped up against a red cola machine, I watch Butter stick his hand up into the air for a question that's surely out of line.

"No," Benny says with a troubled sigh, "this will not affect your retirement plans, Butter. I can assure you."

Butter puts his hand back down on the table and smiles a greasy smile. He always gloats about his retirement, like we should be jealous of frittering away the days at home until we suffer a massive coronary.

Ron then asks, "What about the rest of us?"

"Most of you will get severance packages."

"What are they going do with this place?" Ron asks.

"In a joint project with Detroit Edison, the City will recover and sell the landfill gas to generate energy."

There's a short pull of silence. The fact that we've all lost our jobs kicks in to gear. Everybody is antsy, writhing in the cold metal chairs, hemorrhoids abound.

"Come on!" Ron chuckles and puffs a puff of air from his crooked mouth, his teeth jagged. "Ain't no one gonna believe in that futuristic science fiction horseshit."

In response, Benny nods to one of the EPA agents standing in the doorway. The man's coat says Ruddy. He has a brick-top forehead and a fine pleat of acne on his cheeks. He's Frankenstein without the plugs in his neck.

Ruddy steps up and says, "It's true. Riverview Energy Systems will capture and convert the methane to generate electricity with two gas turbines."

I remain silent. We all do.

Ruddy goes on to give us a speech, the kind some people practice in their mirrors late at night after gargling mouthwash. The speech is all about staying green. Reduce. Recycle. Reuse. Act locally, think globally. I'll bet he has a t-shirt in his closet that says 'Recyclers do it over and over and over again.'

After the meeting, we file out of the break room and Benny tugs at my coveralls, pulls me aside. "You going to be ok, Touhy?"

"Sure." I think about my next job. CAD design? Mill and lathe? Prostheses development?

"What are you going to do?"

"I've got a future in mind."

He breathes into my face and says, "This is a good move for the City. It's a good move for you, too. It'll give you the time you need to finish school and think about what you want to do with your life."

I fight the urge to tell him *this* is what I want to do with my life. I fight the urge to tell him I already have stability and repetition, like my evenings with Madison, who'll never leave me, never die. Instead, I pull back and look at Benny's face pouting with wisdom.

"You didn't think I'd let you stay here forever, did you? You need to grow. There's a big world out there. You want me to write you a recommendation letter?"

I don't answer.

Benny then puts his arm around my shoulder and pulls me closer to his tits. "This'll give you time to think about my sister, too."

My stomach curls and I can't move my legs. I imagine Rhonda's warm mouth over mine, our bodies clamped together under the covers, and keeping our secret life forever.

"What do you mean?"

"You know she loves you, Simon."

Benny cuffs me by the back of the neck and the onion smell of his forearm breezes into my nose. I try not to think of Benny taking a shower, lathering himself, the blackened pubes choking the shower drain.

"Don't string her along. Do the right thing. Either let her go or love her completely."

It sounds like a Foreigner song but I give Benny a weak nod because he's right.

"Good. Glad we had this talk. Lunch is on me today."

Together, we head back outside and toward the office at the bottom of the hill. We pass through the salted walkways, uncomfortably silent, grimacing and shifting like we both have gallstones. How would it be if Benny were my brother in law?

Before we part, Benny says, "Make sure you check The Cyclone again, Simon."

I salute like a soldier and say, "Yes, sir," and walk on out to my 4-wheeler. Suddenly, I turn to Benny and say, "You think you could get me a job with EPA, too? I hear they have good benefits and a union."

Benny laughs and his head skulks, inspecting his clipboard for a diversion.

I actually didn't know he'd gotten a job with EPA until this moment. It was a lucky guess. Instead of answering me, though, he points to the slope with his ballpoint pen and says, "Just make sure you clean the back of The Cyclone before you go tonight, Simon."

The next day, I sneak back into the Highlands and toss Madison into the Dumpster. It's sad how she gets swamped under all the medical supplies and stringy egg filaments, but I realize this is a good place for her, even if I don't recycle her. She is, regardless of our relationship, discarded trash, and I have no practical use for her. Not anymore.

Most likely the garbage pickers will rumble through here tonight, scoop her up and toss her in the back of their broken-down trucks. She'll get to dance with the other heaps of collected metal. Later she'll get shucked and sold like any other piece of scrap, then forgotten without anyone knowing how she made even a few people happy.

Or maybe she'll get plucked out specifically. That would be nice. Perhaps one of the pickers has a heart, a fondness for metal limbs. Perhaps they'll clean Madison meticulously and paint her toenails. Perhaps they'll enjoy the cold touch of her steel calf like I did.

Afterwards, I clean out my locker and leave Riverview Highlands for good. Four years I spent at this place. I thought it would be more difficult leaving. I thought I would pine for the debris, the hum of the snowmobile between my legs, the curvature of the slalom hills on a cold winter's day. But I don't. I might not realize it now, but working here has probably prepared me for something more important, a future perhaps.

In the parking lot, I start up my truck and wonder about Ron and Butter. I struggle to see their future, though I'm sure it'll involve the basics of engineering. Maybe Ron will work for his brother at the auto body shop. Maybe Butter will retire and build a time machine out of his pilferings from the landfill. Maybe we'll occasionally get together at the bowling alley in Wyandotte and have beers and listen to the balls skidding along the hollow floorboards and reminisce about our time together at Mt. Trashmore.

Before I even look up from my steering wheel, I'm at Rhonda's house, a brick bungalow the color of adobe, the color of the setting sun in cold desert evenings.

I pause in the cab of my truck, nervous. I've never met her parents. I've never been inside the house before, though I've seen all I need from the outside windows. I've watched this entire family eat dinner behind the shade of their maple tree on numerous evenings. Rhonda's family eats dinner like any other family. They politely pass the salt and pepper. They laugh over the steam of creamed soups. They discuss the day's events over stalks of asparagus with melted pats of margarine.

I ring the doorbell and Rhonda opens up the door. There's a warm, healthy glint to her eyes and she cracks a smile that melts me.

"Hey," she says.

"Hey," I say.

I lean in and inspect the inside of her home: the welcome mat, the coat rack, the family room being used exactly how a family room is meant to be used. I see Benny on the couch reading an EPA pamphlet. I see Rhonda's father on the recliner watching television, dozing, crumbs and stains galore. I see her mother in the kitchen, standing over a pot that emits gray fog, stirring. And that's when I smell food so sweet and so luscious that it makes my mouth water.

I look again at Rhonda, her eyes vibrant. It's been a while since I've seen that look.

"Come on in and join us, Simon," she says to me. "We're just about to have dinner."

And I do.

Freezer Burn

The freezer full of meat in Goose's garage bothered Tuck because the meat went untouched year after year. Inside there were huge hunks of freezer-burned venison, flanks of beef, and filets of lake trout. Every hunk was packed tight, wrapped in plastic wrap, and covered in tin foil. They were properly labeled and stacked according to date.

It seemed a shame to him, but Goose simply liked to hunt and fish, and there was always excess.

That afternoon, while drinking beer from the can—the crisp metallic taste lingering on their lips—Goose worked on his 1972 Pontiac Firebird Trans Am as Tuck sat on that warm meat freezer and watched his friend work. Tuck was a good listener. He had honest eyes that were the color of laundry detergent.

Goose groused about his wife. It was the only way the guy knew how to communicate. "I know she has ADD," he said. "But she can't even keep the house straight."

It was a nice afternoon. A hazy dusk had settled around the neighborhood while Goose hunched over the car, the hood open like a hungry mouth, his hands deep inside the bowels of the engine, twisting and turning.

"Is it that bad?" Tuck asked.

"Have you been in there lately?"

Tuck looked at his friend's tall frame slouching with gravity, his work pants worn and ragged with swirls of grease.

"Not lately," Tuck said.

"There's a reason for that." Goose found a pair of pliers that pleased him and then pointed them at Tuck. "I want a divorce. And I need to move out of this town."

"Move where?"

Goose whisked at his beer. He often told Tuck his dreams of waking up alone in Washington State, or building a log cabin in the woods of Oregon, feeding off the land.

"I hear Oregon is beautiful."

"You *always* say Oregon."

Goose exhaled. "Yet here I am."

And that's the way this went. Ryan Tuck—with his ungainly feet crossed over one another, his face darkened with a shadow of stubble—would sit on that warm freezer of meat, Indian style, and listen to David Goose spew, his face laggard and bored by evening's end.

Tuck couldn't understand why Goose disliked his wife so much. Nancy was pretty in a burned-out way. She had blonde hair, dark roots, and a chalky face with pink glossy lips. In high school, Tuck had asked Nancy to the Fall Harvest dance, but she'd already accepted Goose's invitation. What stuck with Tuck is *how* Nancy had refused. She'd reached out to touch his arm and then pouted her lips as if to say, "I feel sorry for you. I really do."

"I can't stand the relationship," Goose said. "It's deteriorated."

"Women." Tuck wiped his mouth. "They're a different breed."

At this, Goose stood erect and encouraged his friend. "Tell me more, preacher-man."

Tuck waved his beer can like he was at a podium giving a lecture. "Once you accept the differences between men and women," he said, "your life will become much more manageable."

Both men were buzzed. Not drunk, but light in the head, wordy. They continued the routine and talked about quitting their jobs, leaving their wives, buying cars, and, lit by the cruel desperation that someday their life would be simple, what it'd be like to win the lottery.

"I'd get the fuck out of Detroit," Goose said. "I'm so sick of these winters. I'd go to Hawaii and send alimony checks to Nance and the kids."

Tuck glanced at Goose.

"I'm not a degenerate, Tuck."

"I never said you were, my friend."

"I'd buy a bigger house, too. I hate to see my boys cramped in that bedroom." Goose paused. "I'd still be their Daddy and I could finally get them some decent schooling, some decent clothes. That's something my father never gave me."

Tuck watched Goose look to the streets. The neighborhood was called Ecorse, which was a blue-collar collection of misfits and miscreants. Ecorse sat on the cusp of Detroit's city limits and there was always trash in the streets near Goose's house. A junkyard sat at the end of the road and made everything greasy and oily when it rained.

Then it was Tuck's turn to fantasize.

"I'd quit the grocery store," Tuck said, a swishing glow in his eyes. "I'd march into the Shop-N-Save, turn my keys over to Hastings, and spit right in that fucker's face."

Goose laughed. "Come on, Tuck," he said. "You love that job."

Quitting *was* difficult for Tuck to imagine. He thought changing his life would be akin to racing down the highway and suddenly throwing the gearshift into reverse. Tuck imagined the transmission dumping into the street, coasting to the ditch, the car on fire.

Tuck unflinchingly continued his dream. "I'd buy a '62 'Vette and drive to the end of the world, which, as we all know, is California. Anyway, I'd stop at the water's edge and stay on that beach until the water sucked me down."

"That's beautiful," Goose said.

"Thanks."

"It's too bad we're both stuck here for life."

On the way home that night, instead of driving aimlessly the rest of the evening, avoiding his wife, Tuck hit the grocery store and got a different brand of whiskey and a road map. He splurged on the Rand

McNally and skimped on the whiskey, an off-brand with a disheveled owl on the front cover of the bottle.

The next morning, Tuck got to work on time. Always to work on time, as his wife drove him out early with her incessant questions:

"Did you pack your lunch?"

"Did you send the electricity bill?"

"Did you wash your teeth?"

Wash your teeth?

Tuck had never heard it put that way. He didn't hate Elizabeth, but he didn't like her, either. She was too religious, and he didn't know how she became this way. He'd look up and she'd be dashing off to a church function or Sunday mass. She must've repressed this fanaticism while they were dating, he thought, while making love in the backseat of his car or on the swing set of their old school playground. She wasn't so religious with her panties hitting the dirt, telling her future husband to "Fuck me there, fuck me right *there!*"

After they married, Elizabeth started seeing the face of Jesus Christ in a bowl of spaghetti or the Virgin Mary on a Pizza Hut billboard.

"There she is again!" she'd scream as they whizzed down I-75 toward the Bingo hall. Elizabeth played every Wednesday night. She never won. Proceeds went to the church. Tuck could never see these clandestine figures, though he genuinely tried.

"I don't see anything." Tuck would squint.

"She's beautiful!"

"It looks like a motor oil stain to me!"

Elizabeth preached about piety, the word of God. She quoted passages from the good book, and answered her questions aloud with, "What would a good Christian do?"

With Elizabeth, Tuck could not have the same conversations he had with Goose.

"What would you do if you won the lotto?" he asked Elizabeth that night. Tuck never asked such questions of her, and, immediately, he wished he hadn't.

Elizabeth had the face of a cabbage. It was round, pale, but oddly shaped, bumpy. "I'd first take care of the kid's future," she said proudly. "Then I'd pay off the mortgage, and give some to charity, the church."

"Wouldn't you have any fun with it?"

"Fun?"

"Travel the world? Clothes, fur coats, fancy cars?"

"But isn't it more blessed to give than to receive?"

Tuck stopped in mid-bite of a bland meatloaf. "You're missing the point," he said.

"You know what the bible says, dear."

"Why would I know what the bible says?"

"It says: 'Every man according as he purposeth in his heart, so let him give; not grudgingly, or of necessity: for God loveth a cheerful giver.'"

After the kids were born, Elizabeth lost interest in Tuck. She had long ago lost interest in sex, too. She didn't need sex. She had God.

Thus, Tuck always got to work on time.

The Shop-N-Save opened at 8am. Tuck was there early to open the doors for the butchers and stock boys, who would enter through the back door with white aprons and leave a bloody mess, gristle in their fingernails, smelling like copper. Tuck's pockets jingled with keys. He made deposits and the schedules for the checkout clerks.

Tuck complained but secretly enjoyed the responsibility.

Being there so early in the morning, Tuck often found himself alone in the Shop-N-Save, where he would stare listlessly into the meat section, losing himself in swirling daydreams. The meat was healthy and red. The cellophane was sealed tight and kept everything fresh. Today he had more thoughts of leaving his wife, driving to California, dying on the beach while the tide licked his feet.

During lunch, Tuck sat alone at a wooden picnic table and studied the road map. By the end of the break, a smudge of peanut butter was smeared across Nebraska, and a dusky ring of vending machine coffee hovered around the expanse of Wyoming.

With a red highlighter, Tuck meticulously colored a route across the country. At the other end of the map, he darkened a spot near the Pacific coast. The red ink soaked through the paper and stained the wooden table like blood. The place was called Eureka, and it was right near the Redwood National Park.

That afternoon, Goose excused himself from Tuck and the garage and the metal stink of the Trans Am and, for some strange reason, made a special trip into his house.

Goose was exceptionally drunk and Tuck could hear him stumble through the lava rock near the front walkway. The front storm door then opened and slammed shut. All afternoon he noticed Goose had been distant, his mind wandering.

Tuck feared something terrible about to happen, and so he sat on the meat freezer and waited for Goose to return, as always.

Moments later, he heard Nancy scream from the front door.

"Get out of here!" Her voice was obnoxious, full of hate. Nancy never wanted Goose inside the house until dinner time because she had a hard time concentrating on the kids and dinner and the soaps and the phone ringing and *Jesus Christ did I leave the stove on*?

Then the 'slap' came. The sound was distinct, loud, and it shattered the silence of an otherwise quiet neighborhood. Tuck's stomach turned like he had ingested curdled milk. Goose had never hit his wife before, at least not in front of Tuck.

Tuck wanted to get off the meat freezer and hide.

When Goose returned to the garage, his face was red, his eyes were glassy, and he didn't say a word. He went back to work and ignored Tuck, who was sitting there, waiting, always waiting for Goose to return.

"Everything all right?" Tuck asked.

Goose silently tinkered with the carburetor and then threw his wrench across the garage, the metal end clanking into a garden trowel.

"This thing never gets fixed! The engine idles too damned high!"

"Take it easy."

"This car never leaves the garage, man!"

Tuck waited for his tirade to subside. After the episode, Goose continued to get unusually drunk. Tuck watched him drink beer after beer, his Adam's apple constricting, jumping, the thirst never ending. Goose finally passed out in one of the lawn chairs they'd set up in front of the garage, the cooler of beer between them.

Half sober, Tuck happily sat on his lawn chair and watched the neighborhood come and go.

Charlie, the black mailman with the purple tongue, delivered mail like any other day. Herbie, a 40-year old mentally challenged paperboy—who never really delivered papers because he wasn't really a paperboy, he just carried old flyers and inserts from the garbage and dropped them on random porches—sailed down the street on his bicycle, the tires warped, his bell ringing in the summer day behind him.

At 7pm Floyd Jackson arrived home from the line at the Cadillac plant. Floyd slammed the car door and stood, stretching after a hard day's work. He was tall, lanky, with gray hairs on top, almost glittery with its sheen. His nose was sharp like a shark's fin.

Floyd noticed Tuck and waved to his neighbor from across the street. After a moment of awkward staring at each other, Floyd then yelled, "Trans Am start yet?"

Tuck jumped from his slouch, surprised. Floyd waved occasionally or maybe nodded but normally gave Tuck and Goose the high hat.

"She starts, but she idles too high." Tuck tipped his beer in Floyd's direction, a jovial gesture he thought. "I'm just waiting for Goose to wake up so we can adjust the carburetor."

Floyd snorted and shook his head.

"What's so funny?" Tuck asked. Tuck thought this an honest

question. Maybe Floyd knew something he didn't?

"I think you need a professional mechanic to look at that thing."

"Think so?"

"That car's been in that garage for years now."

Tuck bobbed his head like he agreed with Floyd. But he didn't. He had only realized Floyd was patronizing him and didn't know what to do about it.

"I think we'll manage."

Floyd chuckled, his tone thick with mockery. "Good luck."

This comment made Tuck's chest burn, and without thought, he called to Floyd sweetly, "Oh Floyd?"

Floyd turned around.

"Go fuck yourself!" Tuck said, and then stared hard at Floyd. Excitement welled up into his throat. Tuck wanted Floyd to say something, anything. One peep and he'd race across the street and throttle the fucker.

Floyd grimaced, shifted his weight, uneasy in the situation. Without a word, he then turned and went into the house to his wife, Charlotte, a stocky bulldog-like woman who barked orders at her husband with incisive malice. Deep down, Floyd's wife was a lesbian.

Everyone liked Floyd and Tuck couldn't understand it. Floyd was the type of guy that always gave someone like Goose and Tuck a hard time, whether in high-school or the local bar or the playground. At the block party last year, Tuck had overheard Floyd telling his kids, "They're just a couple of grease monkeys."

Tuck was the only one who heard Floyd make the remark, and he didn't have the courage to do anything about it then. He didn't want to make a scene. People were in a festive mood.

A half hour later, Nancy opened the garage door. Tuck turned back and waved at her like a passing conductor in a freight train. Her emergence on the scene was odd because dinner was still an hour away.

Tuck inspected his friend's wife. She was confident, brimming with something most people called hope. She wore cut-off jeans and a shirt that said 'Bitch' on it. Her chest was round, perky, and she had a weird smile pasted across her puss. "Tuck?" she said.

Tuck got up from the lawn chair, the metal end scraping the ground like a mechanical claw. On his way over, he spilled beer on his wrist and sucked it off his skin, the hairs salty and fizzy.

"Is David sleeping?" Nancy stood in the doorway, uninterested, aloof. She leaned out into the garage, hanging onto the doorjamb, clinging on for fear of getting her feet oily.

"He's taking a break."

"How's the car?"

"We had her purring today."

Everyone knew the car would never run right, even Goose and Tuck knew that. What else would they do if it did? What purpose did they have except to work on a car that never got fixed?

Tuck moved closer. "Once we get her running, we'll take you and the boys out for ice cream." Nancy wasn't enthused with ice cream. Something else was rolling around in her head. She focused on the distance, then refocused on Tuck, a bent curl around her teeth.

"Listen, Tuck." She put her finger on his chest and twirled, the nail scraping his thin Def Leppard t-shirt. Tuck remembered that pout. "I need help turning on the shower."

"Sure thing, Nancy."

The next day, Tuck found himself staring at the meat section at work after Nancy had seduced him. He didn't do anything to stop it. Never even saw it coming. Following her upstairs, looking at her behind, Tuck remembered that he felt sick, crooked on the inside.

He'd seen this kind of stuff on cable television, even pornographic movies. Tuck had once rented *Fucking Your Best Friend's Wife, Part II* and thoroughly enjoyed the movie, but he never thought he'd be doing this to Nancy. Maybe he fantasized, but he never pined.

And unlike the skin flick, Tuck was sure Goose wouldn't actually like seeing his wife screwing his best friend, nor would Goose jump out of the closet and join in after catching them. That would be unnatural. Still, during that moment, Tuck expected to hear soundtrack music pumped from the vents of the house. Music he could keep time to.

"The pin on the faucet is stripped," he'd said to Nancy calmly, addressing the situation like a rational human being. But who acts normal when their penis is stiffening?

"David's neglected it for weeks," she said. "Can you just turn it on for me?"

Tuck removed the plastic knob and turned on the water with a pair of pliers. It was a simple job. In the next room, Nancy was singing "A Groovy Kind of Love" by Phil Collins. Tuck moved quick to get back outside, back to that carburetor, back to Goose.

"See if this is warm enough," he yelled over the din of falling water. Nancy came back into the bathroom and Tuck tried not to notice she had on only a bathrobe, half open. The floor of his stomach dropped. Mist from the shower curled.

Nancy fingered the tepid sprays and said, "Little warmer, please." Tuck bent over and twisted the pin. The steam cleared his nostrils.

When he stood back up, Nancy was naked, and he noticed that her nips were a bit warped and sad, but the rest of her was taut and shapely. Her skin white like a wedding cake.

"That should be good," she whispered.

That's when Tuck's mind went black with lust.

The next thing he knew, he had Nancy perched on top of the sink, and his balls were swaying against the cool porcelain. They fucked quickly, furiously, and didn't even bother to look at each other. The act was over before they could really enjoy themselves.

"Tuck? Tuck?"

Tuck now looked up from his gaze of the meat section and found himself clutching the security keys in his hands. Tony Hastings, the regional supervisor, was standing there screaming at him. The prick had a bushy moustache and resembled a bloated walrus.

"Did you know the back door was open?"

"No, I–"

"Jesus Christ!" he screamed. "Anybody could have walked in here!" Hastings' breath smelled like cheap coffee and soggy cigarettes. He had a real sewer mouth.

"But–"

"Do you remember the last time you left the back door open?"

A few weeks ago, Tuck had forgotten to lock the back door and some street bums that usually slept on the back dock entered through the unlocked door and raided the place. Hastings showed Tuck the surveillance tapes the next morning. In fuzzy black and white, Tuck watched the bums as they scurried through the super market grabbing hams, sacks of potatoes, and a few cases of beer. Except for the coiled loaf of shit lying near the cookie display, not much harm was done. It was an honest mistake.

"I should have done this weeks ago," Hastings said. "You're fired!"

"But–"

"Give me your keys, Tuck."

"But what am I going to do?"

"I don't care! Give me your keys and get the hell out of here!"

Tuck unclipped the keys from his belt loop. He'd practiced this moment over and over while staring into that meat section. He was supposed to throw the keys at Hastings, spit in his stupid fat walrus face and drive off to California in a '62 Corvette.

Instead, Tuck handed the keys over with a dead tinkle.

Tuck obviously had time to kill before he went to Goose's that afternoon. Wandering into the mall, he saw a well-lit bookstore and entered. The store smelled like wood pulp and strong glue. He didn't know how to tell Elizabeth that he had lost his job.

There was also the Nancy incident, but that wasn't his biggest problem. It was losing his job that would get Tuck in much more trouble with Elizabeth. The church needed its donations. The kids needed to be fed. The electricity bill wouldn't wait.

Tuck walked the aisles and skipped over authors like Shakespeare and Balzac, names he'd heard about in high school but never read—all those words hurt his eyes. Eventually, he came upon the self-help section and began flipping through Auto Repair for Dummies.

Tuck went directly to the section that dealt with carburetors.

"Can I help you?"

Tuck looked up and saw that it was clerk of sixteen. The kid had a score of embedded pimples on his cheeks and a coarse goatee that seemed to be made from steel wires, the ones used for marionettes.

"No, thanks."

The clerk noticed what Tuck was reading.

"You need help, just ask," the kid said.

Tuck absently waved his hand and lost himself in circuits and reservoirs. The puberty-stricken boy went back and joined another clerk behind the register, then whispered loud enough so that Tuck could hear, "Must be a fucking dummy!"

Both clerks snickered.

Tuck ignored the boys and sat at one of the tables in the café where he began thumbing through the pages. For the remainder of the afternoon, he drank bad coffee and read about the inner workings of the carburetor. The concept seemed simple enough.

Later on at Goose's, Tuck drank more beers than usual and day-dreamed. He was nervous, dyspeptic. It was well known Nancy couldn't hold secrets. She'd told everyone about the time Tuck had asked her to the Fall Harvest. She simply looked guilty. She had a serpentine tongue and eyes that were smirched with a tint of disgrace.

"Tuck? Tuck?"

Goose now stood above Tuck, who was sitting in the driver's seat of the Trans Am, watching Goose fumble with the carburetor, lost in those daydreams.

Tuck wanted to suggest what he'd read in the *Auto Repair for Dummies*: that the secondary's needed to be closed during an idle condition to tune the carburetor. But he kept his mouth full of beer; the warm, steamy burps rising through his nose like a heating duct.

Tuck was also tempted to suggest they both take off for Eureka so that they could find the Pacific Ocean and then wind their way up north and skirt along the craggy coast of Oregon where Tuck could watch Goose build his log cabin and live off the fat of the land.

But Tuck just sat there and daydreamed.

Near the end of the evening, Nancy eventually poked her head out from the garage door. "Dinner's ready!" she yelled.

That's when a stinging sweat began to bead up in Tuck's palms. Nancy had a flirtatious grin, but she didn't even look at Tuck. She ignored his stare completely and concentrated only on Goose like he was the love of her life.

Goose had then waved off his wife. "Do you want to eat with us tonight buddy? You're always complaining about Elizabeth's cooking."

Dinnertime was when Tuck usually split, but he couldn't face Elizabeth now. He wouldn't be able to stand the disappointment on his wife's face. He knew his heart would sink when the crying started. He would die a little bit with each and every plea to God.

Tuck drifted into his daydreams while Goose spoke.

"Tuck? Tuck?"

The windshield of the Trans Am was dirty.

"Tuck? Tuck?"

A constant barrage of bugs slammed into the windshield, leaving a chunky green residue that slid down the glass and hardened into black knots. The sludge was impossible to get off with the wipers.

Tuck now realized he was somewhere in Iowa. He was coasting along I-80 and had just passed Altoona. He took a moment to look at the map on the passenger seat next to the beer and half-thawed meat, his eyes following the red snake to the end. He was years away from California, and a lifetime away from Detroit.

While he raced through those blinding cornfields, the swaying stalks lulling him, Tuck re-lived that dreadful dinner with Goose's family just a few short hours ago.

It happened after the soup course. Tuck remembered, clearly, almost euphorically, when Nancy spilled the blotchy brown gravy into Goose's lap like a dirty waterfall, the excess cascading down onto the carpet and forming a gelatinous puddle.

It was an accident. Just general clumsiness. An honest mistake.

Still, Goose jumped up and screamed maniacally, the hot liquid surely penetrating his work pants, scalding his thighs, chapping his crotch. Wide-eyed and scared, Nancy backed away from the table, her dirty blonde hair pulled back with a red velvet scrunchee. She dropped the ladle in her hand and Tuck noted that, when it landed, it pointed northwest.

Goose seethed, towering over the scene. There was a swirl of fury in his eyes, and rage was ready to burst from his lips. Nancy stumbled toward the china cabinet to escape Goose's wrath. There she pressed her back up against the panels of glass, her hands clutching the wooden sides of the cabinet. She waited, the splinters clawing into her fingers.

The cabinet—a stunning cherry-wooded enclosure with glass doors, nary a distress mark on it, and passed down from generation to generation in the Goose family—wavered for a single moment, then lurched toward the ground.

Before Goose could make an instinctual grab to stop the thing, Nancy was pinned underneath the cabinet. The crash was muted and dull, as Nancy's body absorbed the impact. Tuck thought the sound would've been more animated, like the cartoons when a piano falls from the sky and crushes the coyote.

Goose's boys (both known to be a bit skittish) ran wildly from the room. Goose quickly scrambled to the lip of the cabinet and lifted, his old hernia straining deep within. He got the enclosure a foot off his wife before it slipped and slammed back down onto her.

There was a muffled yelp underneath.

"Shit!" Goose said.

Tuck stood back and waited. There was shattered glass on the floor. Odd pieces of silverware clinked in the hollow depths of the cabinet. A soup ladle banged and a lasagna server tinkled as Tuck watched the commotion, helpless.

"Call 911!" Goose yelled. "Tuck? Help me get this off her!"

Tuck grabbed one end of the cabinet, snagging strands of Nancy's dyed blonde hair in the process. The two eventually pulled the cabinet back to its upright position. Saltshakers and teacups fell to the ground and plunked Nancy's backside. She was wearing a brand of jeans that cowgirls wear. She remained still on the floor, a crumpled heap of flesh. Blood drooled from her mouth and collected on the carpet like the gravy a few feet away. Next week Goose would receive a hefty bill from the carpet cleaners he would pick randomly from the Yellow Pages.

Tuck stepped back again and watched as Nancy's fingers twitched. Goose kneeled to touch her, to caress her, to pull her hair back, but then stopped short, as he didn't want to injure his wife further. Instead Goose gripped his hands, the tips of his fingernails turning purple and then white. "Jesus," he kept saying, wracking his brain. "Jesus."

Tuck thought about his wife Elizabeth and the prayers she'd often recite when one of the kids scraped their knee or fell out of a tree and how useless those prayers were.

"We can't move her, we can't mover her," Goose kept saying.

At the sound of her husband's voice, Nancy began to struggle. Her palms flat on the floor, she attempted to push herself upward.

"No!" Goose yelled. "She's trying to move, Tuck! Do something!"

Tuck's best trait was standing and watching, so that's what he did, his heart spastic, his friend pleading. Every minute was an eternity. Sweat boiled in his armpits.

"Come on Tuck! Do something!"

This caused Tuck to burst at the seams and he bellowed some sort of war cry, all the frustration and shame emptying from his conscience. He then got down on all fours and talked into Nancy's ear, "Don't move, Nancy! Please don't move!"

Goose winced at the genuine sentimentality that suddenly possessed Tuck. Nancy didn't listen. She continued to wriggle, so Tuck adopted an even more soothing tone as he gently peeled back Nancy's hair and whispered in her dainty ear, "Please, Nancy. Stop moving." Tuck began to sob and then stroked her cheek.

Nancy's eyes twitched and found Tuck's. Then her gaze darted back to Goose.

"Please," Tuck whispered. "Just don't move."

Nancy then stopped struggling.

"I think she's ok," Tuck said as he stood and backed away from Goose's wife. He couldn't look at Goose. Instead he kept his eyes on the half-dead woman on the floor.

For a brief moment, the two men watched Nancy moaning in pain. During this interlude, Tuck could feel Goose's eyes inspect him, like he had caught wind of Nancy's scent lingering on his fingers. Tuck bit his tongue. The silence was unbearable.

After what seemed like hours, the paramedics busted through the front door. More abrasively than Tuck would've imagined, they fashioned a neck brace around Nancy's neck and moved her clumsily to the gurney, her dead weight making the wheels squeak.

The paramedics moved fast and shouted to each other in a coded language only the educated understood. While Goose signed the paper-work, Tuck leaned over and checked Nancy's eyes again. They were open and roving back and forth between him and Goose. She attempted to speak, but only a muffled slur surfaced from her lips.

"Is she going to be all right?" Goose begged the paramedics, tugging at one's shirttail. They didn't answer. He then followed the team of paramedics out the front door and to the ambulance, explaining the situation to them, yammering on and on.

Tuck didn't follow. He stayed inside the safety of the house. The storm door closed and quieted the commotion outside. Goose stood at the back-end of the ambulance and bit his lips, fidgeting as the paramedics explained. The lights whirled. Tuck could feel dusk approaching, though the night would never end.

The paramedics then closed the ambulance doors and Goose moved toward the house. Slow and injured, he opened the storm door.

"They're taking her to Oakwood," he said. "They won't let me ride in the ambulance. I have to follow in my own car. You'll have to watch the kids." Goose hesitated, crimped his mouth shut, and fought the tears. "Thank you," he said to Tuck. "Thanks for all your help." He then reached over, put his hand on Tuck's shoulder and breathed in his friend's face. It smelled like moss and potting soil.

Tuck choked back his confession.

After the manly embrace, Goose tapped Tuck again and then headed down the walk, kicking through the lava rock. Tuck stood in the doorway and watched the parties drive away to the hospital, the siren fading in the distance. He was drained. The quietness of the house startled him. More out of boredom than care, he began to search for Goose's boys.

"Kyle? Trevor?" he yelled upstairs. But no one stirred.

Tuck checked the bathrooms and basement. He checked their rooms and the pantry. He finally found the two underneath the bed in Goose and Nancy's room, whimpering.

"Your mother is going to be fine," he promised them. "You guys want some milk?" They didn't answer and both boys remained under the bed, just four eyes staring out at him like scared cats.

Unwilling to convince them otherwise, Tuck headed downstairs and grabbed a beer out of the fridge. While swigging on the suds, he paced the room, the kitchen, and walked around the china cabinet. When the beer was finished, he went to the front window and pulled the curtain aside and almost dropped the beer bottle.

The entire neighborhood was out there staring at him in the window. At the head of the crowd was Floyd Jackson, shaking his head in shame. Floyd put his arm around his lesbian wife, scoffed, and then walked to his house. The others lingered but soon followed.

When the last of the neighbors trickled away, Tuck opened the garage door and popped the hood of the Trans Am where wafts of grease and oil lifted into his face. With a pair of needle nose pliers, he opened the secondary's and started the engine, revving it until it idled smoothly. Tuck came back around, reached under the hood and made the final adjustments to the carburetor. The engine sounded perfect, even.

Tuck scrambled to the fridge and grabbed more beers. He reached into the freezer and took a few hunks of freezer-burned meat, too. Tuck tossed everything into the passenger seat and backed his car out of the driveway. The car was Tuck's now.

As he hit the on-ramp and lifted onto the freeway, Tuck thought about stopping at a rest area later. The ones with a barbeque pit. It was going to be a long trip to California, and he hated to see that meat go to waste.

Fungoo's Hockshop

I'm crab-walking in the crawlspace when I hear my wife Gloria upstairs banging on the hardwood floor with the butt-end of a broom, her voice like a bird choking on saw dust.

"Dad gummit, Duke!" she squawks. "Quit dilly-dallyin' in that crawlspace and sell them rah-fles!"

I give her the finger from underneath the floorboards, and for a moment, this gesture gives me the small satisfaction I need. It sends a warm creek of goodness that settles into my stomach. Then I realize what an unsightly and bony appendage my finger is, and I quickly pull it down to help me crawl along.

With my heart in my throat, I drag out my grandfather's Winchesters (a classic 1938 rifle and a 1952 Model 21 twelve-gauge), my fist clenching the scruff of the leather case like the neck of a dirty alley dog. The good Lord knows I don't want to sell the damned things, but Gloria and I have bills to pay, a life to catch up with. Before I can haul myself out, the old windbag wheels around in her wheelchair and bangs on the floor again, harder this time.

BOOM! BOOM! BOOM!

Dust skitters down from the rafters and dances upon my bald head. Some settles onto the lamp in the corner, making the crawlspace a tad darker than usual, a cruel rust color. Those floorboards need repairing, I think. They sound hollow with dry rot.

"Do I have to take 'em down to the hockshop mah-self?" she screams impatiently.

Gloria, of all people, should know I don't want to sell these rifles.

When I was a kid, my grandfather taught me how to shoot with these guns, and though I'm no marksman, my affinity for them smolders in Gloria's stomach, irritates her like an ulcer.

I can picture her upstairs: Wisps of dye-blonde hair slipping out of her bun, strong arms working the wheels, her stubby half-legs a twitter. It's easier not to reply to such silliness, to ignore her determined yet unwarranted anger. If she wants to scream like hell and break a vocal cord, that's fine by me. I just wish our neighbors didn't have to endure such racket.

"Hush up you rotten crow!" I yell through the floorboards, my blood temperature steaming, unable to resist. I hate myself for participating. But my wife brings out the best in me. The worst, too.

Gloria lost the majority of her legs while working at a stamping plant in Wyandotte four years ago. We live in Melvindale, a strip of industrial cancer-growth on the edge of Detroit's city limits. Without any whining or petty muttering, I help her get dressed every single morning, her legs sewn at the end like fully packed sausages. The poor girl lost her balance and was sucked under some stamping contraption, a huge metal monster with teeth, and that chewed her up good before the foreman could stop production.

Unfortunately, her settlement and disability hardly covers our bills. I've been retired from truck driving a few years now. To get by, I've been selling my family's heirlooms. Mostly old china and Depression glassware, most of which I have no use or sentimental attachment. But it won't be too soon before I run out of trinkets to sell. And then what?

During my quiet breakfast of oatmeal, I was thinking perhaps I could rob the mini-mart on the corner with one of these rifles instead. Pull my old ski mask over my head, shove the barrel down the cashier's throat and demand stacks of cash. But that old ski mask smells like sour socks. I put it on two months ago to shovel the last snow of the winter out of the walkway, and I gagged on little chunks of my insides that crawled up into my throat. Besides, I don't have the heart for robbery these days. Not that I think stealing is wrong.

The problem is I haven't paid the rent in three months. Charlie, my landlord, has been over to the house twice for the money. Son of a bitch is eighty-two years old and still won't die, which would probably leave Gloria and myself a nice permanent place to live. I'm pretty sure Charlie doesn't have any family that would inherit the place. He's owned this house for over fifty years and has outlived everyone he knows.

Our landlord is a somber old man, frail with dusky peanut-butter skin and droopy eyes. There are scars on his hands from all the handiwork work he does around his house, and there's dander falling from his scalp like flakes of white fish food. The old bastard came over the other day and simply asked for what was rightfully his, and I had to turn him down, sell him our hard luck story.

When he left, I just stood there holding the screen door open and burned with crimson shame and I immediately began thinking about what I could sell. Gloria and I have never been on the nearside of well-off, financially speaking, but over the years we've usually been able to scrape up enough dough for the rent.

Thankfully, Charlie's let us slide now and again. He's a good soul. Goes to church every Sunday. Not that he's fanatic in his religion, just dutiful. He's determined to get into heaven, and he's forgiving, too. Gloria and I have stayed in this house for over ten years now.

I back out of the driveway, rifles in tow. With the money, Gloria will pay the rent and then wheel herself to the grocery store down the street. Hopefully, she'll make something good for dinner. Maybe a roast with red-skinned potatoes and a good bottle of wine. Then again, she may just make bologna sandwiches and set a can of generic beer in front of my face, eventually steering herself to the television for a heartwarming episode of Bay Watch.

"That C.J. Parker ain't very bright," she'll say biting into her sandwich, the doughy white bread sticking to the roof of her mouth. "But she's got some big ones!"

Gloria may just let me starve, too. I never know how she will react anymore. Not only is she crass and undeniably cruel, but she's also completely unhinged these days. In all sincerity, I think she's clinically insane. Even her medication doesn't drag her from the deep end.

I set course for a familiar hockshop on 34th and Vernor, near Tiger Stadium. My old friend Fungoo owns the joint. He's Vietnamese or Korean, I forget which kind of chink he is. I guess Fungoo and I are not actual friends. We mainly haggle over the prices of my dwindling ancestry. I've sold him many valuables when Gloria and I were at our lowest, and I trust him for a decent price, or maybe more so than any other hockshop in the city.

In the backseat, I hear the bag of rifles and leftover ammo clacking around as I go over the vestiges of a historic set of train tracks. I inherited the guns when my grandmother jumped into the grave. She had a heart murmur that stopped murmuring. The rifles have been tucked away in the crawlspace ever since. I've never been a hunter.

Before Gloria's accident, I was driving a delivery truck for an elfin cookie company, I won't tell you which exact one. For twenty-three years I tooled around the broken streets of Detroit, delivering cookies to the most rotten grocery stores on the east side. It was a shack-job of a union, but I was able to retire when Gloria needed full-time assistance.

It was a brutally hot and unpleasant summer day when I found out about my wife. I had just finished my route and punched my card when my supervisor Mr. Hastings put a hand on my warm, sweat-soaked shoulder.

"Gloria's been in an accident."

He'd whispered it like he was telling me a naughty secret and then guided me toward his office. I felt like I had done something wrong, but the look on his face said I had already been forgiven. All the guys dressing in the locker room were staring at me with grave eyes and sunken sockets, an uneasy apprehension crawling around in their boxer shorts. They all knew about the accident before I did.

I remember sitting there and waiting, the air-conditioning in Hastings' office turning my uniform stiff and dead-fish cold. His eyes were full of disheartening solace. That was what stung the most, his soiled and hopeless eyes.

"Gloria was crushed… Wyandotte Hospital…"

As my boss explained, I went blank. His words were a puzzle, his voice disappearing and re-appearing. Then there was that blizzard of white snow like the television going off the air. My brain went on the fritz. Next thing I knew, Jared Remy, a young rookie out of Romulus, was driving me to Wyandotte Hospital. Without so much as flinching, Jared looked over and nodded at me, his hair the color and shape of scorched mattress coils, his mouth solemn. That was the exact time Jared expected me to wake up, and he too had that same practiced look of a solemn funeral director. Neither of us would last at this job the entire summer, but I could recognize that face in a line-up anywhere.

While racing to the hospital, the rush-hour traffic cleared magically. The trees on the side of the highway swooped by and tried to stop us, but Jared was too fast and too agile. I'd trained him that summer and he took to it like a duck to water. He had the gift.

I relaxed and looked out the window, trying to eliminate Gloria from my mind, hoping that maybe she was D.O.A., her arms listlessly swinging from the gurney, gravity working its wonders. Unlike other men I knew—men who despised their nagging, cheating, gin-soaked wives—I loved and cared for my Gloria very deeply, but I didn't want a wife that was damaged beyond repair. At this age people are like used cars: you either salvage the wreck or you junk it and try to get Blue Book value from the insurance company.

Meanwhile, the clouds snaked across the sky and flirted with me. For the first time in years I wasn't in control of that truck, or in control of anything, and I realized that being a passenger felt pretty damn good. That feeling didn't last. When I saw the automatic doors of the hospital opening and closing, I was filled with a thousand needles of dread and remorse because I knew my wife was alive. By the time I found a doctor who knew what was going on, they had stabilized Gloria's vitals. She had gone into shock.

After many cups of vending machine coffee and an apple pastry that tasted like glue, one of the doctors ambled over and explained to me that my wife was very lucky.

"What do you mean?" I asked.

The doctor was a bright-eyed and bushy-tailed man. His pupils looked like swishing tadpoles. He was older than me and enjoyed his job entirely too much. He thrived on people's misfortunes.

"The machine in the stamping plant was very, very hot," he said and stabbed his ballpoint downward into his palm, intimating a clean break. "This helped cauterize her legs. The heat from the machine acted like a soldering iron."

"I see," I said, though I had never used a soldering iron. "But how does that make her lucky?"

"This cauterization was the only thing that saved her life."

I'm sure Gloria would agree with me now when I say her life wasn't worth saving. At night, she often wishes aloud that God should've taken her when he had the chance.

I began holding up convenience stores soon after Gloria's accident. They were small jobs, no big deal really. But there was a gap between my pension and the settlement money, and the trinkets my family left behind would only fetch so much. Mostly, I held up crummy Arabic joints that sell liquor and skin mags to the local minors, so I felt I was doing society a favor.

I'd storm the glass doors and wave around an unloaded .38 and usually come away with a couple hundred dollars. Strictly register cash, nothing from the safes. I didn't want to dawdle too long and run the risk of getting caught. The cash was never that much, but enough to bridge the gap and let me eat.

I figured no one would suspect an old man like me. And they didn't. Before turning in late at night, the house empty and cold, I'd catch some of the stories on the news. There was always some poor cashier telling everybody that a strapping black lad pulled off the caper. Turns out I'm a 6'4" black fella with an afro and a penchant for violence. I ran with that description. One time I called a cashier—a meek little Pakistani girl with a set of the most beautiful ruby earrings I'd ever seen—a "jive turkey." I then smacked her on the head and took some 40-oz. beers before I left. Later, I poured the beer into a couple of plastic cups behind the shed in our little garden, to keep away the slugs.

I've never told Gloria about my crimes, though I'm sure she would have just thought me an imbecile. While she was in the hospital recovering, doing that useless re-hab, I would sit silently at her bedside with these lies buried deep inside my belly. Guiltily, I'd comfort her and wipe her brow with a hanky when the pain became too unbearable.

Without words or warning, she would awaken and always end up reaching for the morphine drip at her side. It looked like a portable doorbell. All she had to do was push the button and the throes of misery were flushed from her system. She would dive into a world that didn't exist to the rest of us. Her eyes would reel back into their lids momentarily, then she'd cringe and stiffen and slowly ebb into a pile of inert exhaustion for a few hours.

I would sit and watch her until she resurfaced, hoping she had found something inside of her dreams that made life worth coming back to consciousness. But that never happened. You could see the disappointment in her face when she realized where she was, what had happened. She would always startle awake, look at me briefly, her eyes hangdog and tired, and then she'd reach for the button again.

We didn't talk much throughout those weeks, but we never

talked much anyway.

On the way to the hockshop, I drive by a huge landmark in our life. The Ford-Wyoming drive-in movie theater is where Gloria and I first met. The year was 1950 and it was the grand opening of the Ford-Wyoming. Some friends and I were there to watch *The Man from Colorado* with Glenn Ford and William Holden, a silly, hacked-up western with lots of gunfire and horses. The price of admission was a little more than two bits.

It must've been the magic of a whole new experience that brought us together. Seeing a movie under the stars, the fuzzy crackle of the speakers on our car windows, the dust and smell of gravel. All these foreign influences spawned an itch for Gloria's plunging neckline and amorous breasts.

During intermission, we locked eyes in the concession line. She was standing with a group of girls none of us knew. They were from another high school on the classier north side of town. I gripped my hot dog nervously and listened to the projector reel spin like a drunken bee. I thought maybe she was a married woman. She seemed older than her friends, and she had a look of resiliency about her. The mustard and salty meat made me thirsty, but I finally worked up the bottle to strike a con-versation. There was no other way than to just walk straight up to her.

"Hello." I tried to be as polite as I could. "My name's Duke."

"Duke?" She glowered for a moment and then rushed me away from her friends, not out of embarrassment or shame, but out of confidentiality. "Are you southern by chance?"

Her accent had kicked in, a thick twang I'd easily recognized.

"Born in Burnsville, North Carolina," I told her proudly.

She smiled, her cheeks scrunching up, her skin like that of a new-born piglet. "I was born in Johnson City. myself."

"That practically makes us cousins."

We both guffawed at that one.

Turns out she wasn't married at all, but a pure southern debu-
tante instead. Gloria was a prim and proper-looking lass on the outside.
From day one she had been raised to marry a prominent textile owner
or something of that nature, but when the deal fell through, her parents
picked up and moved to Detroit for the booming automobile industry.

On the inside, howver, Gloria was a completely different person.
She was fierce, scabrous, passionate. With her high-class attitude, she
belittled everyone around except me.

"Let's get outta here." She looked around at the crowd as if
something stank. "These people make me sick."

For some reasons, she took a liking to me right away. She laughed
constantly and she always had a devious smile curling at her lips, which
took the edge out of her cruel and biting words. The old gal was dotty, to
be sure, but it took me twenty years to realize that I mistook that trait for
spunk and vivacity.

We ditched the rest of the movie and our friends and walked up
Michigan Avenue to a blues bar called Annie's Blue Dress, which is now,
I think, a cathouse. John Lee Hooker played on the juke and we drank
whiskey all night until the bar closed.

"I think I like you," I'd told her. It was a daring move.

Gloria clicked her tongue and said, "Right back at ya, babe!"

We didn't really talk much after that. We just sat at the bar and
sipped the sharp whiskey, staring at each other through the mirrors on
the other side of the bar where the wonderful liquor bottles sat. We were
watching two strange people fall in love.

When Gloria and I got back to the drive-in, all my friends were
gone, hers too, and the front gate was locked-up for the night. Even the
ticket-takers and projectionists had deserted the scene. I ran up to the
fence and grabbed a hold of the links like some kind of deranged convict
seeking freedom. I could see my father's 1948 Ford Coupe in the empty
field of speaker towers, the screen bone-gray and silent.

"I can hop that fence," I told her and pointed toward the gate.

"But what about getting the car out? I don't have bolt cutters or anything in the trunk."

Gloria was busy putting on a thick layer of lipstick. I was already juiced with the love-bug, but what she did next certainly sealed the deal. After dusting her nose, she closed her compact and marched right up to my face, so close that I could feel her breath and see where the patches of red wax filled the grooves of her full, pouting lips.

"Why don't you just drive through the fucking fence?" she said matter-of-factly.

I looked over at the car and then at her again, and without another word, that's exactly what I did. I scaled the fence, started up the engine, and drove my father's car right through the front gate. A couple of broken headlights and a banged-up front bumper later, Gloria and I were making out in the front seat of my father's car like tomorrow would never come. And to me, tomorrow never did come.

After physical therapy, my wife came back home and I stopped the robberies. I couldn't have the police banging down my door with an invalid in the house. Quitting was tough because I enjoyed the rush, the feel of easy cash, and the power of wielding a gun. It erased all my pain, much like the morphine that penetrated my wife's half-body. I've been looking for a similar feeling ever since, but you can't recreate anything like that, even with synthetics.

Soon after she got settled at home, Gloria's fits of anger started. She'd always been a bit of a crackpot, and quite irascible, but her moods took a tumble for the worse. Coming so close to death—and not achieving it—had soured her. It made her feel like a failure.

At first, her tirades were isolated incidents. Little things would set her off: the meatloaf would be charred, or the buttermilk was too thick, or it was the dishes sitting in the sink for days, stinking and festering. She would spit at me or upend her plate or smash a juice glass into the wall, all the while screaming bloody murder. And I admit, I couldn't run our household very well. I tried, but everything got sick or died.

"Look at this place," she'd scream. "All the plants look like fucking chemo patients!"

For weeks on end Gloria would sit and stew in the bedroom and just watch television. Daytime soaps mostly. I'd set up the television stand and bring her carrots and celery and a strong glass of sun-brewed iced tea. Sometimes, when the yelling became unbearable, I'd crush up a heavy tranquilizer or pain killer and sprinkle it into her tea. That would put her down later in the afternoon.

"Why did I ever marry a bum like you?" she'd whisper under her breath when I'd leave the room. Sometimes I let those words hurt me. Other times, I didn't.

From the soap shows Gloria began to acquaint herself with concepts like vengeance and deception. She became poisonous and spiteful like the characters on TV. She'd lie about misplacing my vitamins or what she did with the money I'd give her. Every minor incident was blown out of proportion and we'd end up having nasty and often violent fights. Once, after she ran over my foot with her wheelchair—the fragile little toe-bones crushing into one another—we ended up on the floor wrestling in a bed of glass from a lamp I threw at her but missed. That lamp belonged to my parents. It was an antique and worth a week's pay.

"I bet I kill you before you kill me," she'd said, breathing heavy, rolling to her side and inching her body up against the dresser drawer.

"You're on," I told her, picking shards of glass out of my palm.

Gloria began to resent me for being able-bodied but inept. I began to resent her for ruining our dull, ho-hum lives. Before the accident, we were blockheaded, bored, patiently waiting for the inanity of retirement. Life was going to be great, just lying around and listening to the ballgames in the late afternoons, Gloria out in the garden tending the cucumbers and watering her hydrangeas. But that fairytale never happened. Instead, she became sickened by the smell of flowers, nauseous at the sight of my face.

I, too, became malevolent. I was like the arrogant father who stole the baby on that one show she so dutifully watched, *Life and Love*, and I simply didn't give a damn. I'd even thought about putting her away in some kind of home that cares for nasty invalids like her, maybe visiting every once in a while and bring the poor girl some magazines and fruit baskets on her birthdays and special occasions.

But I don't have the heart for that kind of underhandedness.

What sticks in my craw the most is that Gloria was unable to provide me a child during our marriage. I've tried to make her feel bad about it on many occasions. I know that sounds harsh. Neither of us is right, and I've never met two people who are more undeserving of anything fortunate or worthwhile. Children wouln't have changed that.

I drive around the city for a few hours, avoiding the inevitable. By the time I get to Fungoo's, the night is swelling to a fine purple. I'm sure Gloria is wondering where I am. I'm sure there's an empty hunger rattling in her stomach, too, the sting of hatred in her calloused palms from continuously rolling back and forth in her wheelchair.

I take no pleasure in torturing my wife. It just comes natural. We've always had an implacable knack for suffocating one another, but afterwards we'd always reconcile and fall in love all over again. We were schizophrenic with our affections. When dawn broke, we'd make breakfast and start right for each other's throats again. It was a wonderful cycle, one we became accustomed to. But we no longer revisit the process of falling in love again. We just fight, and we have separate bedrooms.

I enter the hockshop and I'm hit with the smell of dead lobsters. It makes me think about how Gloria always comments on the way I stink when I come home from Fungoo's.

"You smell like rotten fish, Duke," she'd say. "Or should I call you Stinky Fish Head?"

Most of her comments were childish, what I took to be signs of affection, and we'd laugh them off. Sometimes, when we were younger, we'd get bottomed-out drunk and end up making love all night.

Inside the hockshop, a bulletproof glass partition separates the customers from the employees. The place is empty and quiet. There are a few lonely souls shopping the bottom of the barrel for a cheap gift, or perhaps they are retrieving that wristwatch after saving their ass on a double-or-nothing bet from the local bookie.

The smell brings back the hollow pain of selling so many heirlooms. Underneath a glass case is a set of coins I sold for the down payment on Gloria's new wheelchair. We couldn't afford the electric one, and we never did follow-up on the payments for the one she has now. I stopped sending the checks because I didn't think the company would send around a repo man for an unpaid wheelchair.

And I was right, they didn't.

"Why don't you just sell the coins?" Gloria had said in that familiar, yet unpleasant and stern way. That bitch knew I didn't want to sell the coins, but she persisted until I gave in. They were from 1913, the year my father was born.

The sight of Fungoo makes me realize I'm about to be robbed of more memories. But there's not much I can do. He approaches the glass and I speak familiarly with the old man, errant whiskers under his nose and chin like gray wires.

"What you got for me this time, Duke?" he asks, crossing his arms, sticking his hands into his armpits. There's a thin glossy smile peeking out from his greasy face, which sends my anger and regret deeper into the fire, not to mention his broken English.

"A shotgun and a rifle," I say.

The old man peers through the glass and his eyes widen. It's piqued his interest, and for good reason: weapons are a big seller here. Every gangbanger on the streets of Detroit has one of Fungoo's specialties: Buy one handgun and you get half off the destruction of the serial number. No questions asked.

"Tell me about them."

Fungoo likes the stories behind my commodities.

"They're in good shape, Fungoo," I tell him through the glass partition. "I inherited them from my grandfather."

I go on to tell him about their history and paint the words thick with sentiment. I open the leather case and look at them for the first time since I'd buried them in that crawlspace. Although they're antiques, they look practically new.

Through a metal door, Fungoo eagerly steps out into the lobby with me. With a wincing face, he hoists the 1938 rifle out of my hands. He then palms the barrel and opens the shaft, all the while squinting and inspecting the merchandise.

"Hmmmmm," he hums. "Classics, eh?"

From where I stand, I can smell the gunpowder, which sends me back years where I can see my grandfather standing in the middle of his land in North Carolina, showing me how to hold the rifle in the nook of my arm. That summer was like no other. I remember the buck of the shotgun against my shoulder, his scrubby land filled with booze bottles, rusted-out lawn chairs, and makeshift cigarette urns all over the place, the dead tree stump that sat over in the corner near the barn, pockmarked with years of ammunition.

I can remember the Nolichucky River sitting sixty yards south through the brush. The river runs across the western tip of the state like the crooked neck of an asphyxiated witch. When all was calm you could hear it whooshing by, the currents slipping in and out of the jagged rocks, the constant and lulling sway of the tree limbs.

My grandfather was a seedy and slit-eyed man and always had a glowing butt at the end of his virulent mouth, the sour smell of tonic in his hair. Under his drunken supervision, I plucked two cans off the tree stump and broke a bottle that same day. My grandfather had been impressed, and said that I had natural instinct. That was maybe the last time I ever impressed anybody.

Feeling low, I spruce it up and tell some lies to Fungoo, just to hike up the price and sweeten the pot.

"I need the money for my wife," I tell him. "She needs to have another operation, the poor girl. I don't think she'll ever be the same again."

He inspects the shotgun next, cracking the barrel down and splitting it in half. Fungoo looks through the steel cylinder. He's quiet, as cold as they come.

"And having no use for them," I continue, "I've finally decided to sell the damned things."

"So I see," he says, not looking up.

"I was keeping them in storage for my son…"

Fungoo snaps his head up. From years of quarreling and negotiation, he knows my history, my stunted life, all the downfalls. He sees right through me. This wracks my stomach.

"And as you know, I don't have a son," I assure him. "No sir, I have no son… and that means he'll never pick up the thirst for marksmanship or hunting."

I look down at the ground with all the sadness I can muster. This stooping isn't what bothers me. It's the fact that this man doesn't deserve the money he'll make from these guns, or my father's coin collections, or my mother's chest of rag-tag jewelry. These are all the worthless things I would have passed on to my son, if I had one.

"What I'm trying to say is that these guns are in good shape. I'd like to get good money for them. They're valuable to me."

Fungoo doesn't say anything as he hands the shotgun back to me and goes for his pack of smokes in his shirt pocket. The plastic wrapping crackles and he lights up. His cheeks collapse and soon he's squinting through a veil of smoke, his eyes continually wincing. He always does this before he makes an offer. It's his poker face.

"Tree-hundred dollah for both," Fungoo says. "My final offah."

Damn. Not even enough for rent. I look at the rifles and think about how I impressed my grandfather that day, and I realize that I just don't have it in me to fight with this man for another couple of hundred.

Sitting in my car at the mini-mart parking lot, I can hear the sirens off in the distance. They're getting closer and closer, probably barreling down Fort Street at sixty miles per hour, blowing through red lights, dodging Sunday afternoon traffic. The people in the neighborhood will eventually stop opening that can of split-pea soup for a moment and wonder, *What the hell is going on down there?* Then they'll dump the soup into the pot and go back to their lives, the blue flames licking the underbelly of the pan.

I think about the big grins those cops must have on their faces, the saliva rushing into their mouths, gripping the wheel in the white-knuckled anticipation of snagging an armed robber.

In addition to the nervous tremors rumbling throughout my limbs, I can feel the gritty residue from the shotgun blast stinging my fingers. I suddenly realize that the smell—that burnt, smoky scent of gunpowder—will never leave me. It'll always be on my fingers, haunting me for the rest of my life.

Not that it matters much, but shooting the cashier was a total accident. My trigger finger slipped. I got too excited, and before I realized what I'd done, there was a stump of dying flesh on the tile floor in front of me. I didn't know what to do. It didn't register in my brain that I had actually shot the lady.

Immediately I crouched down and apologized to her rather half-heartedly. "I'm… I'm sorry," I said, a glassy puddle of blood burgeoning near the wound. "Is there anything I can do?"

I stood up and noticed that the register was open, but I didn't reach for the dough. It was too late for that. The cashier stared at me with drowsy eyes. She was in her mid-thirties, a portly young ham with a pug nose. She couldn't speak at all. She was gasping for air because I had sprayed her in the chest. Her mouth drizzled with that goopy red ink.

It was all a simple mistake. But you certainly can't explain that to a rabid bunch of cops who thirst for a bloody crime scene like the one I just created. This kind of action is why they joined the academy.

The only thing I can do now is keep quiet and wait for the batons to land upon my head and pray that a judge will show mercy on my soul. I'll probably get ten-to-fifteen, serve a few years up at Jackson State prison and hopefully get out with good behavior. I'll get a job doing laundry. I've always liked the smell of bleach. Or perhaps I'll get to the pen and be shanked in the gut with a rusty fork by a guy named Wendell who's there for choking his wife into a soundless coma.

I'll have to explain it all when the dust settles. That my actions were stupid and uncalled for. I'll admit to a blank-faced jury that I never should've loaded that fucking shotgun. My lawyer will preach incompetence, that it was pure coincidence the only time I go in with a loaded weapon it turns out to be a gruesome case of manslaughter. Victim of circumstance. I didn't mean to kill her.

When the first squad car screeches to a halt in the parking lot, I can still feel the warmth of the shotgun barrel resting upon my lap. Out of the corner of my eye, I see one of the officers drawing his weapon, using the car door as his shield. Smart. Then all the incomprehensible screaming starts, and quite frankly I can only be amazed at their response time. I check the clock on the dash. Just under three minutes. Not bad, not bad at all.

Then the only words I recognize are this:

"Get your fucking hands up and get out of the car now!"

As told, I show them my hands, sticking them outside the open window, and I feel the warm spring breeze tickling my fingers.

This is the part where I begin to think about Gloria, my lovely wife, how useless she'll be without my help, how sick with guilt I'll feel every time she comes to visit me in the joint, if she ever visits.

Perhaps this will be exactly what she needs? To get away from me for a while and live on her own. Maybe, I think, the state prison won't even be wheelchair accessible?

Here comes the first baton.

CRASH WHERE YOU LAND

Lumpy is a no-show for work, which isn't uncommon with the temps we hire at Front Street Packaging. Most of these men are from the scrap heap; bums from local Native American tribes: Skagit, Shoshoni, Quinault. After cleaning up this shit-hole for a day or two, they smarten-up and realize working at a fish-packaging warehouse isn't what it's cracked up to be. They grab a bottle or a needle or a straw and never show their dirty faces here again.

Lumpy is different. On the surface, he's an old white hobo. Honky, as they say, and over the last few weeks, this honky has proven to us there's more to him than eating out of trash bins and substance abuse. He's currently on Front Street's permanent payroll. The man needs us, and, little did I know, we need him. The afternoon rush is a disaster but we make do. The next day, after another no-show, I get the phone call.

"Sean Berry?" the man on the phone asks, and right off the bat I notice an inquisitiveness purebred in cops.

"This is Sean Berry," I say. I'm standing in my office, the day's invoices tucked deep into the nook of my armpit, the gassy breath of forklifts shooting up into my nostrils.

"This is Daniel Devore from the Seattle Police Department."

Daniel's voice has a soft lilt to it. It's as if his wife made him quit the pool league on Tuesdays. He's got that dismal gloom about his tone, too, the kind that tells me he's bummed to spend more time with his seven-year old boy. Ice cream stains, petting zoos, hoof and mouth.

"What can I do for you Mr. Devore?"

I act nervous and make the man work. That's what cops want.

It's a game. I flutter the pages on my desk in absent-minded chaos and cough nervously. Before I became shipping manager of this warehouse (the most responsible position in my 42 years) I've had brushes with the law all my life. I'm on the wrong side of the law for a reason.

Devore gets right down to biz.

"Do you employ a Charles Rogers?" he asks.

"Charles Rogers?" I pause and dig deep. "Sorry. That name doesn't ring a bell, officer."

"You're sure?"

"Charles Rogers. Charles Rogers. Wait—do you mean Lumpy?"

To my delight, the detective gets confused and irritated.

"I'm not sure of any aliases he might have," Devore says. "But Charles Rogers is the man's Christian name. So, I'll ask again, one more time, does Charles Rogers work there or not?"

"I believe Charles is on sabbatical."

"Sabbatical?"

"Thesis work," I say and think that hump could be anywhere in the Pacific Northwest right now. Whether I have or whether I haven't seen Lumpy in the last two days is beyond the point. It's never good when cops call, and I usually skirt their questions and exercise my natural instinct to cover for guys in my trench. I now imagine Lumpy's unshaven mug next to me in that foxhole, the sting of napalm in our eyes, both of us battling trench foot, him asking me to lead the bastards astray. He might do the same for me.

"Is there a problem, officer?"

"Mr. Charles Rogers jumped off the Bremerton ferry yesterday morning. We found a Front Street Packaging check stub in his wallet."

Devore's words hit me hard and my stomach tightens as if I'd choked down a handful of walnuts, shell and all. I get an image of Lumpy floating in the Sound; a bloated porpoise, his lips soaked blue like he was sucking on toilet bowl cleaner.

"Is Charles dead?" I reel back, make myself distant, and pretend

I had nothing to do with Charles' death, but I wasn't so sure that I didn't. I thought this phone call would have me picking the prick up from the drunk tank, his breath smelling like rotted leaves, and later watching him toss up rotgut wine onto the cement outside my car door. When you're around drunks often enough, they seem to need favors of this nature.

"I'm afraid so."

Devore then explains: The ferry was full of early-morning commuters, one of which saw a man (presumably Lumpy) dive headfirst into the icy, black pond. Before anyone could toss him a life preserver, he disappeared into the early morning fog, swallowed whole.

"Hypothermia," he says. "Puget Sound Coast Guard fished him out a few hours ago."

"Poor son of a bitch," I say, suddenly dyspeptic.

There's no real reason for making this any harder on Devore, so I tell the cop what I know: About a month ago, I found Lumpy sleeping out on Front Street's back dock one morning like a discarded bag of garbage, gnats swarming. Instead of booting him off the property, we gave him a job. He was homeless and had been camping on the back dock three or four nights a week. The guy turned out to be a hard worker, and Katherine, the owner of Front Street, has a soft spot for hiring hard-luck cases, men on the rebound.

"I've got a favor to ask," Devore says.

"Of course you do," I say.

"Could you come down and identify the body?"

I stall and conjure up an excuse, but my well is dry. "Why me?"

"Everyone we contacted is dead, in jail, or in a mental facility."

Again, I draw a blank, an empty register.

"You were his manager," Devore continues. "Probably closest thing to family he's got."

After a long drone of static, both of us growing uncomfortable, I concede. It's the very least I can do for the guy, and I'm accustomed to doing the very least.

"He's at the medical examiner on First Hill," he says. "Meet me there in an hour."

I hang up and file the invoices and arrange the day's deliveries.

Before heading out, I call and awaken Katherine at home and tell her about Lumpy.

"You're kidding me?" she growls like a bathroom sink clogged with muck. There's not much empathy in her voice, but underneath she's wounded. I picture her entwined in silk bed sheets, a sleep blindfold pushed up around her head, hair matted yet grizzly.

Katherine is a dwarfish woman who looks like she should be spreading make-up on old ladies at a trashy mall, a heavy perfume-squirter. She also runs a sweatshop next door to the fish-packaging warehouse, but overall, she's a good soul. Katherine only hires from a distinct crew of foreigners, misfits, cretins and ex-cons like myself. We're a cheap labor force.

The Chinese people she "employs" in her sweatshop next door put together cardboard partitions and work for $5 an hour, sometimes more, sometimes less, but mostly less. The Chinese speak no English, and they often cram ten family members into a one-bedroom apartment in China Town, and they smell like weird fish.

Eventually, I broach the Lumpy subject with Ray, my assistant at Front Street. When I leave, he'll be in charge of the warehouse for the rest of the afternoon, which doesn't entail much: poker with the day laborers, chatting up the truckers, and feigning interest. All in a good day's work. "I've got some bad news about Lumpy, Ray," I say as I approach.

Ray stops scribbling on his PO order. Unlike my light skin and frumpy body, Ray is tall, black, and oddly stained, like Orson Welles when he played Othello. He has that same staged beard and that same painted-on darkness, except that Ray is born-again; a Moor with the passion of Christ. We stand near the truck bays with errant delivery drivers waiting for their trucks to be unloaded, forklift fumes coughing out and staining the concrete walls.

After I explain Lumpy's death and its sordid circumstances (which doesn't really seem to surprise Ray), the only thing he has to say is, "It's a shame Charles couldn't find God." Ray then tsks his tongue between his thin teeth like he always does.

"It's a shame Lumpy couldn't find anybody, Ray," I say. "Let alone God." I then bite my tongue and remind myself, in the guise of outward respect, that his real name is Charles Rogers. Ray and I called him Lumpy because he had a cyst on the crown of his forehead the size of a newborn's knotted hand. We never asked, but we had our theories.

"He's a hydrocephalic," I once joked. "Water on the brain."

"I think he got stung by a hornet," Ray countered over the din of forklifts. We'd often park next to each other and chat when business was slow. "It must've gotten infected and never healed properly. I have a cousin in Olympia who's got the same problem."

The knot, depending on Lumpy's mood or time of day, fluctuated and breathed like the gills of a fish. Sometimes the bugger was small and calm, but when he got angry the thing bulged out like a swollen beet.

"Maybe he got it in jail?" I said another time.

Ray, too, has spent time in jail. Armed robbery. Drugs. The works. He's got a real family now, kids scurrying around in pajamas, tucking them into bed, a wife that makes him pot roast. Ray doesn't talk about the pen much, but his eyes are a dead giveaway. They're brown and greasy like timid mice, the only characteristic that will never leave him.

We all have stains only ex-cons notice. Me, I'm missing my right pinky finger, which I lost during a work program while serving time in the Hamtramck Correctional Facility in Detroit for involuntary manslaughter. Who knew a simple fistfight would wind up with the other guy bleeding to death in a ditch? Not me, you can bet on that.

We'd been refurbishing abandoned houses that day, and I remember that it felt good to be outside doing work like real men instead of squabbling around in a hot laundry room like scullery maids. I lost my concentration and that coping saw got the best of me: rusty blade, infection, amputation. When I go to bed at night, I can see that dead finger sitting in a cup of ice, the bone sticking out like a mangled worm. The docs couldn't save him.

After my second stint in jail (a fertilizer bomb test gone completely awry) I left what little family I had and hoofed it on out to the farthest corner of the world in my mind. When I stepped foot in Seward Park in Seattle—a 120 acre patch of forest land on the Bailey Peninsula —I felt like I was at the end of the earth, hidden in one of its many nooks and crannies. That's when I felt I finally had a home.

Wheeling over to the King County Medical Examiner, I try to convince myself that Lumpy was an upstanding citizen, a man of virtue, morals, all that jazz. This proves difficult. I hardly knew him. I have, however, been told that people are good deep down, no matter how damaged we are on the outside. I delude myself, make the sentiment stick.

Over the course of the last few weeks, Lumpy had moved on from the odd jobs Katherine gave him (cleaning up the back dock, sweeping the warehouse, stacking pallets) and began driving a forklift for the Chinese next door. He was still temporary, he was still drunk, and he was still sleeping on the back dock, but his experience working as a longshoreman in Long Beach made him extremely valuable.

I went out to the back dock and kicked his feet every morning for work. From underneath a blanket of cardboard, Lumpy would lurch forward and glare at me with his red, gluey eyes. He would then caress his misshapen head, mumble incoherently and clean up in the bathroom, punching in for work with a pasty yawn.

Because Ray and I were so busy with the "legitimate" side of Katherine's operations, we didn't have much contact with the Chinese, or Lumpy. But, every once in a while, he'd come over and fill us in when business was slow, tell us stories, his cyst bristling.

"Those guys are crazy," he'd say about the Chinese immigrants.

Lumpy would always have a steaming cigarette in one hand and a cup of gashouse coffee in the other. He was a chain-smoker, flipping one cigarette into his mouth after another, the good tarry ones.

"Know that little fucker Lin Yong?"

"Which one is that?" we'd ask.

"The one that looks like the rest," he'd say, jerking his thumb over his shoulder.

"What about him?"

"Bastard was arrested for shooting squirrels in the middle of the God damned city."

"Squirrels?"

"He's been to jail *twice* for shooting squirrels!"

And then he'd laugh with a hoarse death rattle, choking on his damaged lungs until tears came to his eyes. Even the Chinese immigrants Katherine hired were tough-luck cases.

"Suppose those guys eat them things when times are tough. Or maybe they was out just having fun? Hell, I've eaten squirrel before."

"They're rats of a different name!"

"They ain't too bad. Little gamey, but not bad."

Later in the rainy afternoons, staring out the front bay doors, losing ourselves in the boggy, broken streets in front of the warehouse, Lumpy would get more serious and sentimental. He wanted to feel the plight of the Chinese. They were heroic to him. They'd survived dissolute poverty and had flourished after the long voyage across the sea.

"Those chinks will do anything to get out of that country, Sean," he'd say. "You know half those guys were shipped over in a container illegally?"

We knew. Last year, the port of Seattle found a container at Terminal 18 with a slew of illegal immigrants from Hong Kong inside. Three were dead and had deteriorated like rotten peaches. Illegal immigration in this port was a big problem. INS would show up at the warehouse once in a while and snoop around. They would ask the Chinese questions through an interpreter, scribbling in black handbooks. Their investigations never amounted to much, but it always put us on edge because we employed a lot of these stow-aways.

Eventually, Lumpy got back on his feet and stopped drinking and rented an apartment over in Bremerton, which is a shitty little Naval town on the other side of Puget Sound. He took the ferry into Seattle every day and fed the seagulls that hovered around the deck, throwing crumbs of stale bread into the air from a brown paper bag.

We were all on track, a one-way ticket to respect. We recited and preached each other's stories. I remember Lumpy telling us one afternoon that he'd lost his mother and grandmother a year ago, and then his brother in a car crash out in the Sierra's.

"We were pheasant hunting and drank a lot that day," he'd said. "Next thing I know, the truck is face down in the ravine and my brother isn't in the cab of the truck." He then whistled and made a motion with his thick-tissued hand like it was his brother's body shooting through the window. "BANG! Right through the windshield!"

Lumpy said he spent the next few months hitching his way up to Seattle, stopping in every boon-dock town and drinking until his face grew yellow. Instead of the Betty Ford clinic or the nut ward, he flopped on our back dock and waited for me to kick him in the boots. "Crash where you land," he'd said. "That was my motto."

"You ever consider the Lord's help?" Ray had once asked.

Unlike most born-agains, Ray isn't too pushy about his beliefs. His preachings of the Lord are like a helpful hand he holds out in case someone needs it. He did the same with me. The key is to stop the courtship early. Tell him, politely, that God didn't make the cut.

"I can't say I trust the Lord right now, Ray."

"Jesus is always there if you need him, Charles."

"Sure he is."

No one wanted to push.

After proving his salt, Katherine placed Lumpy on payroll. It was a path all of us took. She was building a competent fleet of defectives and wanted only a few commitments: stop drinking, stop sleeping on the back dock, and show up to work on time. It was that simple. Lumpy had been straight for the last three weeks and you could tell because his eyes were no longer hazy or jaundiced. He'd waited patiently for his chance and was bursting that day Katherine let him in on the good news, his eyes aflame like he'd won the lottery. "Man, ever since that accident in the Sierra's, not one soul has given me such an opportunity." Lumpy then looked squarely at Ray and said, "No one. Not even God."

This made Katherine look pretty good. It made Lumpy look good, too. God, on the other hand, well, let's just say his jumper had been catching a lot of iron.

As it often happens, things changed without rhyme or reason. Lumpy had grown to moping around the warehouse, and he was often difficult and pissy when addressed. Two nights ago, I'd locked up the warehouse and slapped him on the back. "You're doing a great job," I'd said. "Keep up the good work."

I hated to play the bit of caring manager, but Katherine had asked me to boost the guy's self-esteem, inflate his morale. She's been to seminars on this stuff.

Lumpy thanked me and grinned as we parted, his gums the color of an irritated clay pot. "Yeah, things look pretty good from down here."

He had a tender tone of thankfulness to his voice, so that's why I was surprised to see him and his girlfriend an hour later in a broken-down bar I visit after work on occasion. I'd cleaned up my life after my stints in jail, but never stopped drinking. It was never a problem for me. I simply kept a mellow buzz and avoided trouble. When I beat that man to death in Detroit, I wasn't drunk, and I didn't start it. I just finished it.

As I walked into the bar, I spotted Lumpy's hobbled body from across the dark room, his eyes sickened with drink. He noticed me immediately and waved me over.

"We're celebrating!" he yelled and raised his foamy glass.

"What are you celebrating?" I asked.

Grabbing me around the shoulder, Lumpy pulled himself closer. "I'm celebrating the end of my sobriety!" His breath was boozy and warm, and his greasy nose had grazed my cheek. I watched him take a swig of his beer, his mouth smacking, savoring the taste. "Whooee! It's been weeks since I've had a drink!"

A pint of watery beer and a shot of rail whiskey arrived in front of me. I strangled the shot glass and hoisted it into the air, the cool contents sloshing onto my fingers.

"Cheers!" I said and slammed back the drink and felt the liquor spread into my tummy like warm moss growing on the side of a wall. We then drank solidly together for an hour, trading quips about jail.

"Terrible food," I said.

"Awful," he said.

"The rice was slimy and had bugs in it."

"I couldn't sleep on those beds."

"I lost twenty pounds when I went in."

"Me too," he said and slapped his flabby belly. "The sex is good, though." Lumpy then nudged my elbow and said, "Just kidding, buddy."

I wasn't so sure that he was. I did know, however, that he was busy getting trashed. The whiskey had him frayed at the edges. He bounced between friendliness and downright meanness. Soon he was flipping the bird to patrons for no reason and tossing pretzels on the ground, stomping them into a mealy paste, and calling the bartender a phony.

I was uncomfortable. I thought about the word 'enabler' and tried to drown that word with alcohol. I got drunk, too. Later, after taking a spill from his barstool and landing on the floor with a thud and a giggle, Lumpy screamed at me when I asked him to calm down.

"I will not calm down!" His sheened nose grazed my ear again.

I didn't know why he was yelling, and I tried to forget it, but he wouldn't let it go.

"What is the matter with you?" he said to me and hopped back on the stool like a rodeo cowboy. "I'm just having some fun."

This sudden bitterness turned the switch in me, and I simply decided not to care about the man anymore. I gave him a flit of my hand. "Carry on," is the only thing I said to him.

Sloppy, hardcore drinkers like Lumpy were part of the reason I left my hometown, and I was good at pretending nothing was wrong. You can ask all the family and friends I left back in Detroit. They'll tell you I was the best.

After we played a lazy game of pool, and after I bought more rounds for him and his current shack-job, Veronica, Lumpy found his humor again. He got chummy and watered up like a fruit. Out of something that resembled kindness, he invited me to his side of the Sound.

"Whatta ya say we grab a bottle, take the ferry and then hit the bars back over in Bremerton?" He retched and almost lost his stomach on the floor. The man was seething at this point. "They got Pai Gow Poker. Place called The Mermaid. Right off the boat!"

I was a loner myself. I'd been in this port for over three years now and still found it tough to make friends and meet women. I guess Lumpy had recognized that in me and wanted to cling. None of us, Ray included, ever talked about the magnetic pull that Front Street had, but I think we all realized how far we had come just to work at this dumpy little fish-packaging warehouse in Seattle.

I felt bad about turning him down. It might have been the first time Lumpy reached out to someone. I could see there was no solace with Veronica. She was just a bar hag and only worried about the next drink, a stiff lay. I bet she was a real brute in the morning, too.

"Come on," he begged me. "Veronica works there. We can have a few on the house and finish off the night at my place."

Though it would have been ridiculous and fun, something I could never again conjure again in a million years, going back to his place was what scared me most. If I went, I would stay, and I couldn't stay.

"Nah, I don't need a couple of drunken losers to put me back in the slammer." I meant it as joke, but as soon as I said it, I felt guilty. I've never been one to preach. People can only help themselves.

Lumpy's face sagged like a bloodhound. Undeterred, he pulled me aside and said, "Don't worry about anything. I got it all set up." He then made a motion over to the pool table behind him and gave a sly wink with the eye just below the cyst. I peeked at his girl bending over the next shot, deliberately showing me handfuls of droopy cleavage. She smiled, her lips curling around teeth that resembled tree bark. Things had gotten out of hand. "Sorry, pal," I said.

"Come on! Celebrate with us!" Lumpy waved to the bartender and signaled for another like he was king shit. I watched the fed-up bartender shake his head and said something about 86-ing him. "I've got a job. I've got a girl. I've got my own apartment. I have stability in my life."

Lumpy put his arm around my shoulder and squeezed. I noticed his blackened fingernails, the knobby bones inside his skin. With his free hand he reached over and tried to tickle my stomach. I doubled over. "Don't make me beg, man," he said. "Come join us."

That's when I looked him square in the eyes. I looked past the despondency, past the desperation. "I can't do it," I said. "I gotta get back up the hill." I listened to the snap of pool sticks and clicking balls and imagined the lonely but satisfying walk home in the spitting Seattle rain, maybe stopping off at the porno booths for a quick stroke.

Lumpy's warm arm fell from my shoulder and he pushed me away. "Suit yourself then sailor!" He said the 'sailor' with a lisp, insinuating that I was queer or weak, I couldn't tell which. Perhaps both. He parked himself at the bar and downed another shot. I could see the dark, dreary place these drinks were sending him. This was my cue. I put on my coat and placed my hand on his shoulder, tightened my grip.

"You should slow down on that stuff, Charles," I said.

He scoffed and looked at my reflection through the bar mirror and nodded, as if he understood. "Fuck it," he said and switched to

CRASH WHERE YOU LAND | 107

bravado, signaling the barkeep for another. "Crash where you land.," he said. "That's my fucking motto."

I finished my drink and walked out the front door. From the street, I gave him a friendly wave through the front window and noticed that distant look in his eyes. He gave me the finger and smiled sarcastically, mouthing the words 'Fuck you.'

This made me laugh and I thought all was good.

As I walked home, I tried to consider what he had in mind with him, Veronica, and me, but whatever it was, I wasn't into it. I wasn't going to say anything to Katherine about the incident, either. I didn't want Lumpy to get into trouble on my account. He'd been showing up to work on time and doing his job. That's all that mattered to me. So what if he fell off the wagon?

Obviously, I had no idea the poor sot would never show up at Front Street after that night.

With traffic, I arrive at the King County Medical Examiner on First Hill in the late afternoon. I cut my wheels by a man waiting outside on the steep marble steps, smoking a cigarette, and by the way he watches me, I know this is Detective Devore.

Last year, I'd read a story in the newspaper where this facility had lost an infant's remains, which was big news in Seattle. People were upset. Presumably, the body was either stolen or misplaced, but one thing was for certain: the child was never found again. It was strange because over the past nineteen years, this particular morgue had permanently or temporarily lost a total of five bodies, three of which were from the Green River serial murders in 1984.

I park the car and pray the facility has misplaced Lumpy's body. I didn't want to see the remnants of this man laying on a steel gurney with no direction but down into the earth.

I approach the detective as the lost Seattle sun nuzzles its way through the white cumulus clouds; the orange rays licking our side of the world for a change. The man tosses his butt, walks over, blows out a plume of rat-colored smoke, and puts out his paw. Our hands clamp together like old school mates.

"Sean Berry?" he asks.

"Yes."

"I'm sorry about all of this."

I nod and we hover awkwardly.

"I know this isn't what you want to be doing on such a sunny afternoon," he says and looks up into the sky.

"Just trying to be a good citizen, detective."

Devore steps back and eyes me curiously, his pupils beady and beryl. The man has a stocky chest and a thatch of hair tilted to one side. Probably a bad rug-job, though I can't be sure. I can tell that Devore notices something about me. Just like bums and fellow ex-cons, cops usually recognize us right away. It's a vicious kinship we have.

"You ready?" he says and his breath hits me like air from a deflated beach ball.

"You bet."

We enter the through the back door. The metal door behind us slams shut and we're suddenly enclosed within a cloud of formaldehyde, cold linoleum. We circle through a maze of hallways and I see nurses with vapid faces, orderlies with jailhouse tattoos, and doctors with erections. We're all silent because the dead people want us that way.

We eventually happen upon a chilly room where I see blue feet hanging out from underneath white sheets. There are rows of gurneys neatly divided up like a high school classroom, some empty, some not. Toe tags dangle and flutter. We walk over to the far corner where Devore checks the John Doe tag and then lifts up the sheet.

"This him?"

"Jesus!" I curl at the sight. I didn't even have time to even brace myself. But there's Lumpy's dead, swollen body, which looks like it'd been filled with a series of saline injections. Patches of purple decorate his chest and torso like mismatched Easter eggs. I check his forehead. The cyst is still big and is still there.

"That's him," I say. "It's definitely Charles."

"Good," he says. "We can put him to rest then."

I think about life's weird circles: I'd discovered Lumpy while he was asleep and I'll leave him the same way. I feel like kicking his foot and waking him up to help me unload a rail car full of salt or sweep the back dock or stack some pallets. I want to take him back to the warehouse, punch him in to a place both of us will find familiar, accepted.

Devore drops the sheet. I fight the urge to head for the exit and burst with vomit. Back in the main part of the facility, after the paper work is signed and filed, we then disappear from the scene. No one notices our exit. We don't matter because we're still alive. The entire process of identifying a dead body is all over very quickly.

Outside, I shake the detective's hand and attempt to leave. I want to rid myself of this clinging mess and get back to my life as a lonely warehouse manager in the middle of Seattle. I want to continue to steer clear of old paths I'd found too easy to travel in Detroit.

But Devore is in a chatty mood.

"Mind if I ask you a few questions?"

This makes me leery, but I agree.

"Why do you think Charles jumped off that ferry?"

"I don't know." I scoff. "Wish I knew what made the man tick."

"Did he say anything?"

"Like what?"

"Anything that might've given an indication he wanted to die?"

I think about it. "We all have a death wish," I say. "Isn't that what Freud said?"

Like any normal cop, he wants answers. And like any normal ex-con, I didn't have answers. No one does. I knew very little about the guy, but maybe more than I cared to admit.

"Why do *you* think he jumped?" he asked.

"I honestly don't know."

"Come on. Give me something here, Sean. Give me a theory."

I shrug and think about it and then give Devore my best speech. "Maybe Charles wanted to change," I say. "I'm sure the urge was there. Then again, maybe he didn't feel it necessary to change, no matter what opportunity had been given to him. Maybe this is who he was. Maybe he was a man whose fate was to jump off a ferry and into Puget Sound?"

"Go on," he said. "You might be onto something."

"We all need a crutch, right?"

"A crutch?"

"Yeah. Something we keep around to make life easier to choke down. Hope, God, a warm woman in the sack."

"And?"

"And maybe this guy didn't have anything. Maybe he had no one. Maybe his corner of the ring was empty, and there was nobody there to throw water on the man's face between rounds, nobody to take that drink away, nobody to tell him not to jump off that ferry."

The detective didn't seem fazed. "Well," he says and lights up a square, the tip turning orange. "Having spent years dealing with suicides, I guess all we really have is speculation."

"Unless they leave a note," I say.

"A note always helps." Devore chuckles and looks up into the dark sky. The complexion of the day has suddenly changed. Rain is on its way again. Wet and gray. "The weather doesn't help much, huh?"

I study the swirling clouds. "It's just rain."

"Rain is why Seattle is the suicide capital of the world."

"What happened to Russia?"

"Never mind Russia. This is Seattle."

Devore needles me for another beat. Maybe he senses I'm on the same path as Lumpy. Maybe he senses I might be a little stronger than Lumpy, but maybe he also realizes that the strength I do have probably won't last very long. It never does.

"I appreciate the help, Sean." Devore shakes my hand again.

"Sure thing," I say.

And we leave it at that. No I call you or you call me.

I watch as Devore humps his oafish body into his unmarked squad car, the suspension sagging to one side. I doff my imaginary cap and watch the man maneuver his black sedan through the parking lot, the tires bald and squeaking. He weaves his way into rush-hour traffic. Maybe, I think, I'll see Detective Devore again someday.

Walking to my car, I choke back the guilt. I try to forgive myself for not reaching out to a soul who might've needed me. I try to forgive myself for being so selfish, and I hope that someday I can find somebody to stop me when I'm ready to jump off that ferry.

But none of this will change the fact that the world is full of lonely people like myself and Charles Rogers, and it's not uncommon for some of these people to end up at places exactly like Front Street Packaging.

PADDY WAGON

Week after Erin kills herself, I blow town. I jump on the Dan Ryan and wind my way south on I-55 to New Orleans. Twelve hours later, I'm driving the back roads of Mississippi at 3am with a bottle of Jameson in my crotch. There's indignation in my veins as I navigate dark roads that shift like pools of soot.

Erin did the deed in her one-bedroom apartment in Uptown. The toxicology report said it was a fatal mix of vodka and the sleeping pills I stole from her medicine cabinet from time to time. The brand name of the pills sounded like the name of a spaceship, and I'd take them in the morning to make work more tolerable.

Erin had the gas jets turned to full blast, too. She was determined. She had moxie. We hardly knew each other. I met her at a bar called Tuman's Alcohol Abuse Center. She had hair like enriched spaghetti and eyes that lied. Her face was full of irreconcilable nightmares. We touched tongues before I even knew her name.

Things went on. But before I had the chance to end it, Chicago Police found Erin dead on her kitchen floor. She'd been there for two days—clammy and blue—before a neighbor smelled gas seeping from the towel-stuffed crack of her front door.

The corroded sign loomed in the distance: *Bienvenue en Louisiane*. Just outside the city, I stopped at a Denny's and had breakfast. Fry cooks clinked and clanked their tools on the grill. A troop of transsexuals sat across the aisle, cooing and jeering. The best of both worlds, though I've never been afforded the luxury of either.

With a belly full of bacon and eggs, I hit the Quarter and started drinking again. I soon found out that the bars in New Orleans are like shipwrecks. Warped wood. Creaking floors. People without eyelids darting in and out or moping around the hull like sad catfish.

I also found out there are ghosts in this city, too. They hide in the darkened corridors while the tourists eat the red, oily crawdads. The ghosts laugh at you and they numb your mouth with drink to make sure you don't spread the word about their city.

Tired and drunk, I managed to find a room on the outskirts of the Quarter. A man with a crooked face rented me the efficiency. My floor shared the one bathroom.

"No vis'tors." Native bayou tongue. Bouquet of irritated pimples across his cheeks.

"Shouldn't be a problem," I said. I needed to be alone, idle, to gain perspective.

The room smelled like a dead seagull. I paid the rent a week in advance, which would give me time to settle down and get another pedestrian job. Later that afternoon, a pair of eyes peeped through the keyhole of the bathroom door when I squatted to take a dump. I spat at the eyeball and the eye disappeared. I then heard a pair of hobbled legs shuffle down the hallway.

"Hurry up in thah!" the voice said. "I gotta go."

I would later find out that voice belonged to Curly Bordeaux. Curly's leg had been blown off in the Korean War and he dressed the stump with a blue sock and a broken shoe, its tongue lagging behind like a thirsty dog. The leg was painted a flesh color that didn't match his own.

Later that evening, I went out to the Quarter again and ended up at a bar called Caligula's, a sex joint. There were horses in the back room waiting to be sodomized, but I didn't venture back. Shortly before dawn, I saw some poor tourist get mugged out in the streets. Face in the gutter. I just stood there and watched it all like I was a ghost myself.

I'd gone over to Erin's place a few weeks ago without knowing what had transpired. The relationship, as far as I was concerned, was a dead fish, and I was trying to keep my distance. But I also figured she deserved an explanation in person, which was very mature for me.

When the building manager saw me approaching the stoop, he hustled down the stairs to tell me all.

"Didn't you hear?" Anders said from the top of the stairwell, his chest bulging out of his tight t-shirt. He was Norwegian.

"Hear what?" I asked.

Anders was older. Around 50. He had a moist face and a thick, ashen moustache that probably smelled of herring. Only cops and foreigners have moustaches like that. Anders had seen me coming and going from Erin's apartment. I always said 'hello.' I'm a cordial man.

I thought Anders was making small talk. That perhaps he was so excited because it was such a random yet obscene event in an otherwise quiet neighborhood, and I was about to knock on Erin's door.

"Wait!" he screamed. "Don't!"

"What is it Anders?"

"The police. They were here. They wanted to talk to you."

"The police?"

"I gave them your number."

"You what? What do you mean? What happened?"

Anders cultivated his moustache and then, trembling with confusion, as if he'd just found his mother in bed, cavorting with a woodland animal, he told me about finding Erin dead in her apartment.

"She committed suicide?"

"Looks that way. Poor girl."

"Did she leave a note?"

"She did," Anders said. "The thing was stapled to her finger."

I knew Erin to be self-immolating and noticed she had slowly-healed nicks and scratches down her arm like pink slugs. I suppose she had stories to go along with these scars, but I never asked.

"What'd the note say?"

Anders crossed his arms. "I didn't read it," he said with a huff. "The cops took it as evidence."

Erin had once mentioned Anders had a crush on her. He would dote and show her extra attention other tenants in the building did not receive. Flustered, Anders turned rather abruptly to go upstairs, stopped, and then asked, "Would you like to come up for a drink?"

It was 8am. I had to be at work in a few hours. I said yes.

"We'll drink to Erin." I had noticed his accent was getting more noticeable. Hard 'k's, rolling 'r's.

We spent the afternoon talking about what happened: the police, the coroners, the body bag. Anders had called Erin's parents in Louisville. Anders was obsessed and knew her entire life. I suspect he resented me for not knowing more about her. The two of us drank chilled vodka while he told me about the first time he showed Erin the apartment.

"She'd just moved here to Chicago from some suburb near Indianapolis." Anders put the bottle of Christiana back into the freezer, the dry foggy breath escaping from its mouth. "It was the first time she ever lived alone. Straight off the bus, that girl."

I thought about Erin's pasty face. She had an innocent-enough look to her, kind of plain and pretty, but when she smiled, her thin, spaced-out teeth gave an air of sultriness only girls in porno movies have. I found it rather sexy.

The entire affair wasn't all bad. For a very short while, Erin and I shared a cynicism most people couldn't comprehend. Like me, she disliked organized religion and social gatherings and technology. She evaded her taxes because she thought the world was ending. She told telemarketers she was dead. She didn't believe in much.

This attracted me most. Problem was she had no sense of humor to go along with that cynicism. Erin dwelled on certain subjects, and her sarcasm was too scathing, her rants unrelenting. At least I was able to laugh at how shitty the world was. She never could.

I told Anders this.

"She *was* an angry girl." Anders conceded. "She never did seem all that happy here, but you could tell Erin was relieved when she got here in Chicago."

"What do you mean 'relieved?'"

"She never elaborated, but I think Erin escaped something awful in Indianapolis. I could never put my finger on it."

We all escaped something awful, I thought. Maybe not in Indianapolis. Maybe not in Detroit. Maybe not in Chicago or Seattle. But we've all left something unwanted behind.

Anders talked on as the afternoon turned into evening. Earlier I had called work and told them I wouldn't be in. I listened to Anders and waited. I didn't want to be presumptuous, but I wondered if my name was in that note she had stapled to her finger.

Sarah leached onto me sometime during my second day in New Orleans. She saddled up next to me in a bar called Parker's and smelled earthy like a wet sandcastle. She dressed in hipster rags and had orange locks. It didn't take her long to hit me up for a drink.

"You from around here?" She had lungs full of cancer.

"Is anyone from around here?" I said.

"No." Smoke trailed out of her nose like an oven.

"Then I'm not from around here."

She cranked lime into her drink. Took a sip. "Where you from?"

I didn't want to be from Chicago anymore, though the place would never leave me. "I'm from Denver," I said.

"Good skiing up in Denver. Drugs, too. You holding?"

Sarah was quick. No bullshit.

"No. You?"

"Just some codeine. Want some?"

"Of course."

Sarah dove into her purse and rustled out two pills. I chased them down with a slug of whiskey. My dough was running thin so I suggested a bottle and a walk around the Garden District's graveyards. She couldn't say no because she simply didn't care.

We finished our drinks and shoved off. She felt magnetic. Just as magnetic as Erin felt when we first met. We soon found ourselves strolling through the cracked tombs. I bought us both a bottle of screw-top wine. Red lips from the blood of the lamb. Sunlight lay in shattered pieces along the ground.

I tried opening up. "My father loved cemeteries," I told her.

"What do you mean 'loved' cemeteries?"

"He's a genealogist. It's strictly a statistical fascination."

Sarah had an aquiline nose and brown, craggy eyes that dug into my skin. "Now that's sick," she said.

We sidestepped a vase of fake flowers near a tomb. I took in the serenity. "I'm not sure if he enjoyed the quietness of those cemeteries, though," I said. "Not like this."

I shut my mouth and imagined my father scribbling, stooped over an illegible tombstone, chipped like a broken tooth. His lumpy body and dark thatch of hair. In this sequence, I can see that his eyes are empty, threadbare pockets.

I haven't talked to my parents in years. Not since the riots in Seattle when those damned windows in the downtown streets looked so inviting that I had to kick them in.

I still owe them the bail money they wired over.

The codeine and wine were working. I took a seat on one of the cement plots. Naked cherubs danced the top of the tomb like chubby preschool kids who had eaten too much paste. I poured out to Sarah. It was comfortable, yet not quite right at the same time.

"You know what I like best?" I asked.

Sarah didn't answer. She was lost in codeine.

"I like those new graves with fresh piles of dirt."

I pulled her close and wanted to dump all my rottenness into her.

"I get a kick out of knowing that underneath those piles of dirt are people who died perhaps recently as a week ago." I smiled and hit the juice. "Fresh bodies."

Sarah settled into my arms. The sun was hiding behind the magnolia trees. Everything around us became damp and cool. The sky was purple, like a shade of eye make-up only seen on hairstylists and beauticians and hookers.

After I fingered Sarah to fruition, we fell into comfortable silence.

After talking to Anders that evening, I felt guilty. Our conversation made me feel like I did something wrong. So the next day I stumbled into the police station on Clark and Waveland. If the pigs wanted to talk, I'd talk. I knew the scene well: traffic cops milling about, bad moustaches, even worse haircuts. Potbellies and heart disease.

I told them my name and was shown the way to an interview room. There was a desk, a few chairs and a cold wind blowing through the ducts that hit my neck and made me feel like hiding. Eventually, two plain-clothes cops entered and brought me up to speed.

Turns out Erin's family wouldn't accept the idea her death was a suicide and they were pushing the department for further investigation.

"We're absolutely sure Erin committed suicide." Angel Martinez had brown skin like an organic potato. He sat on the desk and looked at me through a pair of non-prescription glasses that made him look smarter. "But Erin's family thinks something else is going on."

I told him I didn't understand.

"New city, new boyfriend, new problems." Detective Skids stirred non-dairy creamer into a cup of coffee. Skids was middle-aged and had a paunch like an abused kangaroo. He sucked coffee out of his little red straw and pointed it at me. "Read into that how you like."

I shrugged.

"In her final letter, she said she was unsatisfied. Unsatisfied with her parents. Unsatisfied with her boyfriend."

I felt a small sting in my heart. She was in transit to a Louisville cemetery, but Erin had managed to drop the bomb on me before I could do the same to her.

"When was the last time you saw her?" Martinez asked.

I told them about that last night. We had dinner at a Cuban place on Wilson and Wolcott, about a week before her overdose. Erin and I split a bottle of burgundy and picked at our Ropa Vieja. She had just given me what I thought to be an ultimatum in the car.

"Why do we even do this?" Her eyes were wet, glassy ponds of sadness. "Why are we together?"

Again, I shrugged. In our short time, I had never seen her cry.

I wanted to feel stronger about Erin, but I couldn't muster up the courage to do so. I'd read once that certainty and trust are essential in a healthy relationship. I unearthed that nugget of advice in one of the Oprah magazines Erin had sitting around her bathroom. I think Erin read magazines like that because she hated them. Anyway, I had to crap, and I didn't mean to ingest the advice as such, but I also couldn't bear to read the back of the Air Wick canister again. I'd already memorized the warning: "DO NOT puncture or incinerate container." And during those last days together, I'd imagined myself jabbing the can with a pair of scissors over and over again, flinching from the explosion of aerosol, the sweet sticky contents splashing all over my face.

Certainty? Trust? I was only certain that what we had would end as quickly as it had began. And I trusted that outcome.

Erin broke down in the car and I gritted my teeth. Down the street, the champagne lights of the Green Mill glittered without purpose, without meaning. I didn't have a ready-made answer for her, and instead of returning to her apartment for that last grasp, that last swipe at humanity through animalistic sex, I went home alone after dinner.

I didn't have the answers the cops were looking for, either.

"Go home," Skids said. "You're just the unwitting boyfriend."

"But we might have some follow-up questions for you, so make yourself available. Stick around town for a while," Martinez said.

That's when I packed my bags and quit my forklift job.

It was time to get out of Chicago.

The next morning, I awakened in my efficiency to banging on the front door. I didn't answer because I feared it was the building manager coming to kick me out for having Sarah in my room. We'd scampered in through the back door last night after sucking the town dry.

There was more banging. It wouldn't stop.

"Hey in thah!" the voice finally said.

It sounded like someone getting choked with mustard gas. I covered Sarah with blankets and then opened the door slightly. It was the old man with the prosthetic leg.

"Sorry to intrude, but do you have change for a dollah?" He had moles on his green neck and black pouches under his eyes. He looked like the guy from Salem's Lot. I covered my neck and checked the nearest exit if he decided to become frisky.

"I need change for a dollah," he asked again and paused. "You got change for a dollah? Gottah call mah brother tah come pick me up."

"Jesus."

"No need tah bring the good lord intah this, son." His jaw was loose and his cheeks were thin and meager. Down the hall, I heard the building manager's television set, which sounded like the bayou fishing program I saw on television the other day: *Captain Crawdad's Bayou Adventures*. Alligators, herons, water nutria, and other unnamable critters all scurrying across the swampland of the south.

I hurried the man in and the musky smell of chow mein followed close behind.

"Name's Curly." He extended his hand nervously. We shook. His eyes were unable to focus and his leg thumped every time he took a step. *Thump-drag. Thump-drag.*

"Korean War," he said and motioned to his unrealistic plastic foot. "27th Infantry Regiment, Sahgeant Majah Curly Bordeaux. Lots of action durin' mah stay."

"Serious stuff in that war, Curly?"

"Shore. Got caught up in a battle near the Manchurian bordah. Some infested rivah called the Yalu. We had to punch our way out of the mountains near Kuneri. Heavy mortah shells. One blew mah leg apart. I didn't even feel it. I just lay thah, mah leg scattered about like bloody oatmeal. That niggah Cortland saved mah life. Pulled me outta that foxhole, dragged me tah safety. Woulda been left fer dead if he hadn't done what he done."

Curly seemed a decent enough fellow.

"You need a drink Curly?"

"Shore." He then nodded over at the snoring, rumpled bed.

"Don't mind her. She's a heavy sleeper."

"I can't nevah sleep," he said.

I went over to my pants, fumbled through the pockets, and found a dollar in change. We exchanged at the same time, then we went over to the counter and I poured us two whiskeys. We shot them back. I asked Curly to stay and buffer.

"Sorry. I can't. I have tah wait for my brothah," he insisted and moved toward the front door. "He's picking me up for mah birthday."

"Happy birthday. How old are you?"

"73 years young. Born heyah in Nawlins. Charity Hospital. Did mah training in Biloxi."

"If you want, come back later and celebrate, Curly."

He waved at me and shuffled out the door and down the hall. I went over and looked down into the street of New Orleans, my stomach aching from alcohol abuse.

Sarah soon woke up and we sat in our underwear not saying much to each other, fighting our hangovers. Old Satchmo muffled his way through the small clock radio. I asked Sarah to stay, though I'm not sure I had much choice. She didn't have anyone.

And neither did I.

Final night of my week's rent, Sarah and I go out into the Quarter and drink 'til we're good and stupid. If we said anything worthwhile or important or were considerate to one another, we'd have forgotten about it in the morning anyway.

We drank and walked.

We drank and walked and watched the ghosts skittering in and out of the piss-dried alleys and we drank more. We drank and struggled through the crowded mess of Bourbon Street. We drank and breathed in the humidity of a recent thunderstorm. We drank and watched a burlesque show and we drank more.

"What are we going to do for rent?" Sarah asked.

"I don't know," I said. I hadn't even bothered looking for a job.

Everything then whirled, and while dancing in a sea of people on the corner of Dauphine and St. Louis, out of a hopelessness I could no longer quell, I pulled a horse's tail that belonged to a New Orleans mounted policeman. My motions were hindered, slow.

I didn't mean any harm to the horse. I just wanted to stroke the tail, the grainy strands of hair smelling faintly of manure. But I must've yanked the horse's tail a tad too hard because the next thing I knew, I was being manhandled across the street.

Still on his horse, a lumbering and strong beast I soon realized, the policeman dragged me out of harm's way and shoved me face first into a nearby brick wall, which suddenly tasted like a paddy wagon nightmare and a million miles from Chicago.

Sarah gasped and pleaded with the officer. I heard the warbling of the crowd. The whinny of the horse. Then silence. The glimmer of nightlife slowly blurring with tears.

As I was read my rights, I watched Sarah wind down the street, away from the commotion. At the corner, she turned and gave me a sad little wave, then disappeared into the rush of anonymous bodies. I knew she wouldn't be there to bail me out. I knew the "we" wouldn't last.

The cuffs came. The horse clopped its hooves on the cement. I finally got a good look at the officer. He was short and angry with a bushy moustache. Everyone against me had a moustache. I saw his gun in his leather holster and I wanted nothing more than to dislodge the gun and feel its cool barrel at my temple. Smell the powder.

Then I turned and faced the crowd as best I could. I had been exposed. Everybody knew what I had done.

I was a horse fondler and worse.

The paddy wagon eventually rolled up and the cop unhinged the back door. All metal and crisp inside like a refrigerator. I stepped into the container and got situated and that's when I saw Curly Bordeaux sitting across from me, his eyes wandering, his fake leg sprawled out in front of him.

"Curly," I said and sat back. "Thought I might see you again."

Curly sucked at this mouth like there were ice cubes in it.

"What did they get you for?" I asked.

"They picked me up fah trying tah buy crack from an undercovah officah." He smacked his lips. He was in need of a good fix.

I tried to get comfortable. It was going to be a long night.

"No rahpect for vet'rans." Curly gained concentration for a moment. "What about you, son? What'd they pick you up for?"

I looked at Sergeant Major Curly Bordeaux. It was time I confessed to someone. Someone important.

"They picked me up for neglect," I told him. "I ran away from the ones I loved."

"Terrible crime." Curly tsked and put his head back to relax.

"That's just the thing," I said and smiled. "It only gets worse."

"Always does, son," he said. "Always does."

The paddy wagon started up, clunked into gear, and we made our way to the 8th District station.

ALTOONA

"**Y**ou left them out *there*?" The gas attendant looks at you, his coveralls pinstriped, his lapels ragged with swirls of grease.

"Yeah, why?" Your voice sounds incredulous. Suddenly scared, before the gas station attendant can even explain the unknown treacheries of central Iowa, you blurt out, "It's not dangerous out *there*, is it?"

The attendant glances at the buttons on the register and shakes his head. He then addresses you like you're the biggest dipshit to ever exist: "You're telling me that you left your wife and kid out on the side of the highway? In this heat?"

You grab the back of your sweaty neck and stall for an answer, the afternoon's warmth finally catching up to you. "Well, now that you put it in that kind of light…"

This is when you realize it was a bad idea. That leaving your wife and one-year old son out in those cornfields on a deserted road, vulnerable to prey, the radiator of the car hot and dry like the lungs of an asthmatic, was simply a bad decision.

In fact, the entire trip to Colorado to spend your fifth wedding anniversary in a log cabin in the middle of the Rockies was a mistake as well, an ill-conceived idea from the very start. Your wife hates the outdoors. Don't you remember?

You sigh and inspect the soft-drink cooler in the corner of the room, the clearness of the water bottles creating a moment of wayward euphoria, an off-kilter paradise.

You think: *Why didn't I go to Hawaii? Why didn't I leave Jesse with my mom and take Vicky down to the Bahamas? I could be pool-*

side, cupping a frozen fruit drink with plastic swords, the breasts of a thousand different women right in front of you, the waves lapping the sand a hundred yards away.

After hemming (no hawing), you defend yourself.

"But I walked over four miles just to get here!" Your voice is now steaming with anger, your legs trembling. "I can't drag a one-year old kid along the highway for four miles!?!"

This, surprisingly, is a good point, and the attendant realizes it with an uncaring shrug. He nods and breathes deep.

After your explanation, you feel better, but you also can't help thinking about all the seemingly harmless mistakes you've made over the last few months—the ugly, derisive comments you made to your wife, the online affair with Farrah, that anonymous hand job in the back of the strip club lounge during Tom's bachelor party. It all comes under the microscope now. The guilt spreading like a rash.

The attendant—his name tag says Rolfe, though he doesn't look like a Rolfe, who does?—wipes the crinkles of his forehead with a plaid handkerchief. There's a fierce, ugly mole near his left eye. Rolfe looks exasperated by all that's not right in the world.

"The best thing we can do," he says, pointing to a man banging in the adjacent garage, the man's legs sticking out from underneath the belly of an old orange Chevrolet. "Is send Vance here to go out and get them with the tow truck."

"Yes," you say, a crack in your voice from the lack of water, dehydration settling in. "Yes, thank you very much. That would be great."

"Vance!" The attendant looks through the glass door.

Vance keeps banging. The attendant screams again.

"VANCE!"

Finally hearing Rolfe, Vance wheels out from underneath the car, his hat backwards and crooked, his reaction unfamiliar with such an urgent tone.

Broken streets. Abandoned buildings. Wide-eyed vagrants. The city of Altoona is a dump. You are, however, thankful Vance has driven you and your family to the nearest strip of seedy hotels. It's a five-mile jaunt from the gas station where your car is being repaired. Blown gasket. Oil leaking onto the timing belt. A mess. It'll be a cool grand to fix.

"Trust me," Vance says and swigs from a bottle of Mountain Dew, a delicate, home-like friendliness to his demeanor. "You don't want your wife and kid sleeping in the waiting room of a gas station all night long."

Which isn't exactly what you planned to do, but it did cross your mind. Rolfe had promised to have someone work on your car overnight, due to your unforgiving circumstances. You have to be in Chicago by Monday morning for work, and there's no way your boss would let you take another day off.

Cramped in the cab of the tow truck, your wife Vicky now looks at you with a steady sign of agreement peeking out from the back of her eyes, which are the color of blood gone dry.

"Yeah," you say and snort sarcastically. Everyone is worried about the welfare of your family except you. This makes you feel guilty.

Jesse, your one-year old son, starts to squirm and rub his eyes. He's tired, cranky, and begins to cry.

"Awwww! And how old is this little bugger?" Vance uses his best baby-voice, taking his eyes off the road momentarily. For the most part, Vance is a careful driver, aware of the need to drive safely in this special situation, both hands gripped at nine and three. You notice, however, that the floor mats of the truck are covered with white gunk and an assortment of odd-looking seeds, almost like the bottom of a henhouse.

"Jesse's one-year old now." These are Vicky's first words since you blew up at her on the road back there. You remember how it all started. Your wife said, so innocently, too: 'I smell something funny.'

That's all it took: 'I smell something funny.'

So what did you do? You lost it. Went bonkers. Ape-shit.

And really, who could blame you? You were, after all, so

incredibly hot. The crotch of your pants were riding you tight and your back was sweaty and itchy, and you simply couldn't stand any of this vacation anymore. You couldn't stand your wife's small but snide comments at the way you were driving, the way she gripped the door handle whenever you made a left-hand turn, as if readying herself to die.

This had been gnawing at you since you left Chicago.

And it didn't end there. Oh no. You couldn't stand the sour aroma of Jesse's milk bottle, either. Jesus. You couldn't stand the tight, humid air of Iowa. *Jesus!* Those terrible cornfields! And don't forget the crying. The constant fucking crying! The crying and the cornfields! How could anyone think reasonably in the middle of all that corn?

So you snapped. You told Vicky she better shut her goddamn yip, but that didn't help with your release so you continued to shout wildly, raving, telling her to fuck off when she started to protest and then, sadly, you smelled it, too. Something *did* smell funny. Something *was* burning, and that's when an even stronger whiff of grilled plastic and oxidized metal passed under your nose.

And there, at the front of the hood, is where you saw a sizzling cloud of smoke drifting up from the little black crack. Seeing this broke you, and as you began pulling to the side of the road, you almost fell asleep from pure exhaustion, the car fishtailing in the gravel. The feeling was like freefalling, dying.

After an hour of staring at the hot engine (you don't know how to fix cars, despite having grown up in a safe southwest pocket of Motown), not one car passed by on the road, and you made the executive decision to walk to the nearest gas station. In your sandals. Like a jackass.

"I have to go look for help," you said, and your wife gave you that constipated look of disagreement when you told her this plan, but she didn't protest. She knew she wasn't stopping you.

On the way, stamping along the hot pavement, you developed blisters. Bad watery ones. The pus soaking the leather of your sandals and creating stains. When you arrived at the gas station, you entered the door ready to spit nails. You were ready to throttle the first person to cross you. You were seething.

Now, looking at your wife in Vance's truck, you want to apologize. You want to tell her you regret having yelled at her. But you're too stubborn to do that. Besides, it'd be too difficult to do the right thing at this juncture. You clear your throat instead, put your hand on her leg, and give it a squeeze, which is not exactly a weak gesture.

Vicky looks at you, her face gaunt, and, as she turns away and stares off into the winding streets of Altoona, you can tell that she, too, believes this trip was a bad idea. She hates the outdoors, remember?

You then tell yourself, *This is life. Things just go sour sometimes. It's nobody's and everybody's fault.*

The good thing is you don't have to convince yourself—or your wife—that you still love her. You *do* love her, and she knows you love her, too. But you wonder how far you can push this discomfort before it's too late. Like the car, you wonder: What'll be the estimate on the damage?

"Have a good night," Vance wishes you and your family at the mouth of the lobby, a ratty-looking hotel that advertises $29.99 a night, the last of the nines being a six upside down.

"Thanks," you collectively say, and everyone waves back at Vance, including your sleeping son, with the help of your wife's manipulation. Contrary to the way he'd been driving the entire ride over, Vance then screams off, the dust curling up from underneath the truck's wheel well.

You wake at the first sign of dawn. Over in the next queen bed is your wife and son. Her legs are entangled in the white, stiff sheets, and her knees are knobby as ever. You go over, lean down, and smell your son's diaper, which doesn't need changing. Not that you planned to change him even if it did need changing. Just a habit.

You move to the bathroom and let loose with all bodily functions. A heavy stench of urine and gas fills the room. You shake twice because you know what they said about shaking it more than that.

While getting dressed, your wife awakens, looks at you through puffy slits and asks, "What are you doing Steven?"

"I need to go check on the car."

She looks at the alarm clock on the mantel.

"But it's only 5:30."

You look over at the clock, too.

"I know. I can't sleep. Besides, it'll take me a while to walk there."

Your wife hums and rolls over, cradles your son.

"You want some breakfast?"

"Sure," she says.

"I'll be back in twenty minutes." You open the hotel door, a crack of light illuminating your wife's face, but she's already asleep, la-la land.

The streets of Altoona are uneven and full of gravel. There's a band-aid in the gutter, a crunched-up can of malt liquor, old socks. The morning is brisk, a cool relief from yesterday's heat. You hope today will be better, but seeing a shady fellow wearing a leather trench in your path, his face grizzly and unshaven, you think it could be worse.

You begin to cross the street, hopefully unnoticed.

But the man sees you, your escape, and approaches anyway.

"Hey brother," he says, a toothpick in his mouth.

The man's face looks peppered, seasoned with brown flecks of bumpy skin. You think how horrible it would be to touch his face, how difficult it must be for him to shave with all those nubs of skin sitting atop his cheeks.

"Good morning." You keep walking, looking for the nearest fast-food restaurant, the hazy glow of the golden arches. You pass him and the strong stink of spoiled butter hits you.

"Hey, man, hey." The man actually tugs at your shirt from behind. "Listen man, I got this hot-ass girl all set up for you."

You knew it was coming. The pitch.

You stop dead in your tracks and turn around. "Yeah?"

"Yeah. She's over in this hotel room. She's waiting just for you."

You then contemplate what the man with the knobs of brown skin on his face is actually saying. *What girl? Who's he talking about?*

He mistakes your confusion for interest.

"She's all set." He smiles at you. Despite his rugged face, he has marvelous white teeth. He must use the whitening strips and flosses every day. "She's real nice too," he says through those beautiful white teeth. "Got big ol' titties!" The man cups his hands like he has two big grapefruits in them, bobbles them up and down.

You laugh.

"All you need to do is give me fifty dollars and follow me over to the hotel on Grand Street there." The man points down the street and you follow his crooked finger, the morning sky bursting through the saggy remnants of the night.

You shake your head and attempt to shrug him off.

"No, thanks, man."

"Come on! She's a real stunner! She'll do *anything*!"

You stall a moment, as it all sounds like quite an adventure, something you could never again conjure in a million years. But you've got to get breakfast for you and your family. The hunter-gatherer instincts prevail. There's also that five-mile walk to the gas station, and you don't have time for such shenanigans. And you don't have $50.

"Whattaya say?"

"I don't think so, man."

"Why not, brother?"

"Because it's too early for hookers," you say and walk away.

You're the only one in McDonalds, which really isn't a McDonalds anymore. It's now called Ralph's, a de-arched franchise, and they have everything that McDonalds has: breakfast sandwiches, hash browns, weak coffee, bad service. You place your order with the manager, a prissy fellow with a moustache that is dry and uncultivated, like a pinch of hay that's been trampled on by a horse.

"Have a nice day." The manager pushes the tray toward you, his lips a shade of pink you've only seen on women.

You sit at a table, banging your knee as you slide in. You gorge on the breakfast sandwich and regret eating it as soon as the last bite presents itself, the egg dry and flaky, the gristle from the sausage wedged in your teeth. You wash it down with coffee that tastes faintly of dust. You read the local news, the crime blotter. There's a stolen car, a missing person's report, and an assault and battery at a local bar called Pop's.

For the first time in weeks, you feel alone. The sunrise is beaming in through the plate glass windows, showering the mucky floor. You feel good. You relax, breathe out. Then you get introspective about your life, your marriage, this awful trip to the Rockies.

First, the cabin you rented for two grand was a complete rip-off. Each room smelled like something only a vulture could digest. The couch was saggy and old. The television didn't work. The water was rusty. Out on the lake, your only respite from the family, and the fish weren't biting but the flies were. You made love to your wife only twice, once you couldn't even climax. You'd had too much wine prior to performing.

The only fun you really had was wrestling around with your son, smothering him with kisses and throwing him up into the air. That was good. You missed him. You had been working too much, and you were thankful for the time you were able to spend with him.

Also, there were the raccoons.

One night an entire family had attacked the garbage cans on the side of the cabin. Again, your wife tipped you off.

"I hear something," she'd said.

And like a determined soldier, you jumped out in your pajamas in the middle of the crisp Colorado night and shot at the rodents with the .45 revolver you brought 'just in case.' You aimed high, didn't plan on hitting them, and it was a fucking blast.

You imagined the coons were your enemies, a rival gang infiltrating your turf. The bastards had surrounded the house, ready to attack, spread disease. You laugh now at how much joy you took in firing at them, and you remember how disappointed you were as they scampered back into the dark woods, out of harm's way. You'd hoped they'd come back the next night, a special return engagement. But they didn't. They'd learned their lesson.

Your wife had called you a 'maniac' when you came back into the cabin, dripping with sweat, swelling with adrenaline. Your son was crying because of the racket. You knew, however, that he'd appreciate the story later, when he gets old enough. You were proud.

Out of boredom, you now open two sugar packets, dump them into the ashtray, and wonder if leaving your wife and kid out on the road so haphazardly isn't a sign of the near future, some omen revealed to you by a gas station attendant named Rolfe. You've had problems, sure, but they're getting worse and worse these days.

A slew of senior citizens trickles in to Ralph's. They're usually the first ones in the joint, you can tell, and you notice that they notice something out of place, too. Collectively, the brigade looks over at you and scoffs. Point made, they line up and snap and snarl their orders like angry turtles, all ordering the same bottomless cup of coffee.

"And don't forget the discount!" the leader of the pack growls at the manager. The leader is a bald, pink-skinned old man, smooth. "You always forget to give me the senior discount!"

"Yes, sir, Mr. Davies," the manager says.

Obviously, this is their turf, and you decide that you've worn out your welcome and take your leave, exit stage left.

On the way back, you again see the man with the nubs of brown skin on his face. Seems like he's just snagged his first customer of the day, as he's talking through the driver's window of an old white van, which says *Pete's Painting Co.* on the side, the words too scrunched together toward the end, the artist who painted the van had run out of room.

Apparently completing the deal, the pimp jogs around to the

passenger side and, before he gets in, fires an imaginary gun at you, then shrugs like your opportunity has been lost. This saddens you in a way.

Inside the hotel room, you place the greasy bag of food on the table near the phone, the smell of biscuits and sausage filling the room. You hope this won't wake your wife and son. You also hope that the sandwiches won't sink to the pit of her stomach like yours did, but you don't have much faith in that.

It's still early, but it's also a five-mile walk to the gas station, so you decide to head out. You hope by the time you get there Vance and Rolfe will be finishing up with the car. You put on a pair of tennis shoes and grab a bottle of water.

Before setting out, you write a note to your wife, briefly explaining that you've gone to get the car, and that you'll return within a few hours. You tell her to be ready when you get back. You underline 'be ready' and write your name at the bottom, but leave off any kind of sappy salutation.

You close the door and are tempted to go back and scribble in *Love* or *Kisses* at the bottom of the note. Instead, you traipse down the hall and, though you haven't seen her, you fantasize about having sex with the maid cleaning the room a few doors down, her cart full of toilet paper and bleached towels and ice buckets used as ashtrays.

This sex-with-a-maid scenario has always been a fantasy of yours.

You peek into the room that's open and see that the maid is an unattractive lady, not hideous, but plump with purple sweat pants, her eyes spread too far apart from one another. Still, it would be easy to get those sweat pants off, you think. Then, bang, home run.

The first mile goes off without a hitch, and it feels good to be out early in the morning, with the dew from the weeds reaching out and wetting your shins, the sun spreading warmth along your back.

You notice weird debris along the side of the highway: a decapitated doll's head implanted into the dirt; a rusty propane tank hiding in the brush like a silver warthog; an axe handle; a smashed-up videocassette, the ribbon-y guts of which are reeled out and collected in a shiny blob a few feet away.

You think it's probably a sex tape with an under-aged girl or some guy getting fucked to death by a horse. It could be a bar mitzvah, though, or a family birthday, a son's baseball game. Maybe even an actual movie? A classic like *In Cold Blood* or *Rear Window*.

But, you assume the worst. It's what you do.

During the second and third mile, you begin to show signs of fatigue—occasional stars, dizziness, cramps—all stemming from a weak night's sleep.

On the fourth mile, a Lincoln Town Car pulls abruptly to the side of the road and stops, the blinker on the right hand side still blinking as you approach. You think about those poor drifters who disappear in the middle of Iowa. You think about the local cops finding fingers without hands, shoeless feet on the bottom of the cornfields.

Getting closer to the car, you see it's an older man behind the wheel. He has a few splintered suitcases in the backseat. There's also an old microwave, a box of books, a clock radio, some trophies, and an ancient pair of boxing gloves.

"Headin' through Des Moines," the man says though his open window, the air conditioner whirring. As evil as you want him to be, the man has a wholesome face, and his eyes are without any predatory or cruel intentions. "You need a ride?"

You look down the road. Maybe over the next horizon you'd be able to see the gas station. But you wiggle your toes and feel the soreness, the sting. "Yeah, I could use a ride."

You think these will be famous last words.

Opening the door, you think of Charlie Manson, the Green River killer, Ted Bundy. The man clears the passenger seat, and as he shovels away notebooks, fast food wrappers, and a thin telephone directory for Boca Raton, you notice his hands are soft and pink. Once inside, there's the faint smell of aloe or cucumbers, something organic.

You adjust and try to get comfortable.

"I'm headed to a little gas station up the road here," you say.

"Oh." The man is disappointed. "I was hoping for some company. You know, someone on board to help me stay awake. Cure the boredom."

"Sorry."

"That's ok. You're the first decent-looking hitchhiker I've seen on this miserable strip of highway."

You think to yourself, *I wasn't hitchhiking.*

"I notice you got some boxing gloves back there," you say and the man pulls back onto the highway and gathers speed. The old man takes a cursory glance back at the gloves.

"Golden Gloves champion when I was eighteen."

"Wow, a boxer, eh?"

"I peaked early and had to retire at the ripe age of twenty-four." He points to his head. "Too many knocks to the noggin."

You're waiting for the other shoe to drop. You're waiting for him to make a pass at you or start talking about Jesus and join his crusade. But there's nothing. An odd smile, that's it. He is, however, gaining much more speed than you care to admit.

"Where you coming from?" you ask.

"Florida," he says. "Too damned hot there this time of year. I'm on my way to visit my daughter in Utah."

"Is she a Mormon?"

"No, Vegan. Animal lover. Name's Bert."

"Steven."

"You married, Steven?"

You wiggle the ring finger in his periphery.

"Yeah. I was married once," he says with a laugh. "I let her get away, though."

"You regret it?"

"Most days. I miss the fights."

"Really? Most people complain about the fighting."

"Bah. Fighting kept me virile," he says, and then turns to you and speaks confidentially, "Made me an animal in the sack."

This makes you laugh heartily, and you realize this is the first genuine laugh you've had in weeks.

"What about you, Steven? What's your story?"

With a sigh, you tell the man briefly about your excursion, the trip out west, the drive home, the car smoking in the middle of those cornfields. It all comes out in a rush. You then look up and see the gas station off in the far distance. You also look at the odometer and see that Bert's topped out at 80MPH. A flutter settles into your tummy.

"This is it, Bert. I appreciate the ride."

But Bert speeds up a bit more, gunning it to 90MPH. You grab the passenger side door handle and think that maybe this is what your wife feels when you drive, the vulnerability.

"It's no problem," he says in a sing-song voice.

You start to wonder if he's going to speed right past the gas station, lock the doors, trap you in the car and rape your dead corpse. The old man then makes a reach for the glove compartment. *A gun*, you think. *Jesus Christ, he's got a gun.* You picture your escape: a tuck-and-roll into the weeds, some broken bones, nothing that can't mend, though.

"Well, good luck in Utah." You try to keep up everyday banter, just to keep your mind off the speed, the gun. Bert's pink hand finally jimmies open the glove compartment and out falls a mass of business cards. They're three-dimensional: Bert's Oldies, which is the name of his antique shop in Florida.

"We specialize in Fenton glass and Blenko vases."

You breathe deep. The flutter in your stomach disappears as he hands a business card to you, and then he presses down hard on the brake once he realizes he's going too fast.

"Oops. Sorry about that," he says, pulling off onto the side of the road. "I tend to get a heavy foot."

Entering the parking lot, the gravel crunching underneath the wheel well, you swallow your excitement and say, "Thanks, again, Bert. I appreciate the ride."

"No problem at all. And good luck with your wife, Steven. Take it easy on her. She's your wife, after all."

You grab the door handle and look at the gas station, pause and then ask, "How'd you know?"

"A man can just tell. I've taken my wife across country before. It's a real bitch. You fight and curse. But you'll both appreciate it later on."

"Thanks again, Bert."

The old man heads off down the road and you wonder if he'll ever make it to Utah. You picture him falling asleep at the wheel, feel the vibration of rumble strips, see the explosion of the driver's side airbag.

Rolfe welcomes you with open arms as you enter the gas station lobby. He's become even nicer since you first met him, which seems like days ago. You're family now, a good friend. He's downright courteous. Never critical. Always supportive.

"Come on in, Steven!" He looks at Bert's strange car speeding off down the highway. "Hell, we could've sent Vance here to get you."

"Ah, I was up. It's not a problem."

"We're finishing your car right now."

In the garage, your car is hoisted in the air, Vance underneath twisting and turning his metal tools. Vance notices your presence and waves to you. Animated, you wave back like he's your son, like you're Barney or Chuck E. Cheese. You don't know why you're so thrilled, but you can't quell it. You wish achieving this joy was always that simple.

For a moment, you loiter and watch Rolfe as he fusspots around the register, bumping into everything.

"Go on and sit down there," he says. "Have a donut."

Before sitting, you look at the box of donuts on the counter, which says Ralph's Donuts. There are only two left. One is bleeding jelly and the other has the half-sprinkles. A drop of nausea trickles into your gut. Rolfe quickly disappears, you sit on the chair, and the cushiony drone of AM talk radio soon lulls you to sleep.

A dream: Spacey commotion. Floating pastries. Breathing cornfields. Your son on the side of the road. Bert next to him. Your wife in the trunk of his car. Banging. Banging. Banging. You blaze past them all in your car, smoke steaming from your engine.

The horn of your own car awakens you. Vance exits the vehicle and pulls up his saggy coveralls. Rolfe re-emerges from the depths of the back office and you slap down some plastic to pay the bill. You genuinely thank them both. You shake Rolfe's greasy hand way too long and way too vigorously for any man's taste.

They say, in unison, "You drive safe," and you're thinking they both must've rehearsed that line a million times now.

You say something inane like, "Will do."

In the rearview mirror, you watch both men shuffle off into the office, Vance tucking a wrench into the back of his coveralls, Rolfe adjusting his specs. Nice people. They didn't gouge you. They even offered you a discount on the timing belt by locating some coupons in the local mailers.

It's not in your nature to trust people, though, and as soon as they are out of sight, you look in the console to see if they haven't pilfered the change. You check your CDs and the glove compartment. But nothing seems amiss. You laugh at the whole stupid episode. You laugh at what a jackass you've been. Perhaps you've changed because of this? Sure. Anything's possible.

Situated on the highway, you lean back and gun the engine to 70MPH, the pedal soft and forgiving. You have to make sure the car can handle the torque. You don't want to get 100 miles down the road and find out they did a bum job. The car sounds good, though. Better than when you left Chicago, that's for certain.

You exit the highway and roll through the crummy streets of Altoona. You feel un-strange, normal, as if calm wave after calm wave were hitting your feet on the beach. Finally, you're getting a break from the world, a break from everything.

You turn right onto Grand Street and see the string of miserable little hotels situated on the street like hollowed-out skulls. Out in front of the Grand Iowa Inn, you see the van you saw earlier that morning, the one with *Pete's Painting Co.* painted on the side of it.

You pull up next to the van and wonder about all the good times going on in that room. You think about lusty sex and booze and loud music. You wish you could join this world, if only for a moment.

You look around the perimeter of the hotel, check the windows of the rooms, and see if you can't catch a peek of the action, the fun. Unfortunately, all the shades are drawn, the doors are shut, and the privacy tags have been hung on the doorknobs. Quiet.

In the front office you see that the clerk is doing a crossword puzzle, or perhaps writing his memoirs, or a best-seller about a rogue detective investigating a small town murder in Iowa. He yawns a pasty yawn and you echo his sentiment with your own yawn.

That's when you suddenly feel the dark urge to seek out the man with the brown nubs of skin and see if he's got something set up just for you. Hookers. Coke. Unsettling pornography. Whatever. You want the dirty tonic to cure your itch.

You put the car in park and get out of the car. With your arms on the roof, you inspect the street, looking one way, then the other. You're excited, but you see nothing. It's all empty. It's as if no one even bothered to wake up this morning. You feel lost.

Dejected, you get back in, pull the car forward, and approach your own hotel. It's time to go home, you think to yourself glumly. It's been a long day already.

Stopping at what seems like the only stoplight in town, you

see, down the street a bit, the entrance for the expressway. You see and hear cars zooming to and fro. It's a blur of commuters, vacationers, and truckers. All heading somewhere important. All doing something much more interesting than you.

You look at your hotel, and even from here you can see that your wife and child are not at the doorway waiting like you thought they might be. They're probably still asleep and nowhere near ready to go, the breakfast sandwiches uneaten, the diapers unchanged.

It'll be an hour, at least, before you get back on the road.

You look back at the entrance of the expressway as the street light pops from red to green. Time to go, you think, and you step on the soft and forgiving pedal, gathering speed.

Stripped

Two years ago my wife was brained in a car accident. Since then, I get by with cheap thrills. There is no clear line of demarcation, and what constitutes cheap varies. Peeping usually works. Profanity, mockery. I'm a scapegrace. It's in my blood. As kids, we huffed paint thinner and tortured caterpillars, frogs. There was a vice involved. Shame. Much shame. Those poor bugs didn't know their fate was in my hands.

That's been the lowest I've been. I peaked at the spry age of ten. These days, I'm curbing the behavior. I'm trying out the adult thing. Soon you'll see what I mean.

I work at a dry-cleaning warehouse on the northeast side of Detroit, near the Rouge River. Every day the gas hoses *pisshh* and *passhh* late into the evening, which creates an atmosphere like a sweatshop in Thailand. The work never stops and the warehouse smells like burnt people, a crematory. Goebbels would get off.

This is is the part where I'm tempted and the adult thing goes out the fucking window:

Nearing the end of another afternoon shift, while on a cigarette break in the alley, my coworker and best friend Paul says to me through a mouthful of grimy smoke, "We should go to the booby bar."

"Do you even need to ask?" I feign interest. "I'm already there."

The skin joint ain't cheap. I'm not really in the mood, but I concede because I need entertainment to survive. Reality television just isn't cutting it these days.

The bell rings, ending our break. Paul and I watch the rest of the employees form a single file line, a human wick, and march bravely toward inanity. Most are from the Philippines. They look sick. They're very quiet, aloof. I'm afraid of them, and they me.

We flick our cigarette butts into a scuzzy puddle and head inside to finish out the shift.

After Paul calls his wife from a payphone, we make the trip to Atlantis, near the airport. It's a natty grease-spot of a tit-bar. Paul and I have been going since we were eighteen. We're now thirty-two and have faces like weathered brick, splotches of graffiti.

Someday we'll renounce our membership to this group, these dollar-stuffers. We'll step down in lieu of reorganization. Perhaps we'll join the Moose, something respectable.

Paul doesn't want to join the Moose. He says they're just flabby old men in a constant gripe session, mentholated backsides. They put ice in the urinals at the Moose club, too. I've never figured that out. Maybe Paul's right, but I'd still like to get out of the booby bars.

Inside the bar, lights drift about the room. The place feels like a fish tank filled with roving sea-creatures. Legs twirling. Hands fondling. Women upside down on the brass bars. Chimpanzees in second-hand lingerie. Their world is a cage.

"Look at all the BOOBIES!" Paul points to all the representatives. "We got floppy ones. Perky ones. Fake ones," he says. "And how can we ever forget about the members of the Itty Bitty Titty Committee?"

Paul likes them small, firm, like swollen knots. I don't care. As long as they don't look like undercooked pancakes, I'm aroused. As a dancer passes, I catch a whiff of baby oil, which suddenly makes me sad. Dana, my wife, would slap that stuff on her shoulders after a hot shower. Now I yearn for her touch, the clinically proven mildness.

We take seats at a table without shame. We know better. Sitting at the stage is desperate. We may have the pedigree, the background, but we're not like these other humps, these louses. The girls will come over if they're not ill-natured or crabby.

On cue, one with a big dumper approaches our table and plops down on Paul's lap. She burrows her hungry bum into his crotch and chirps: "Do you want a dance, sweetie?"

Paul, as calmly as he can: "Not now, princess."

It's hard to resist getting down with the first girl who approaches. We know the game. We have to play it cool. She giggles and smothers her chest into his face. I catch a different fragrance from this girl. It's like a syrupy fructose from a punch drink.

"What's your name?" she asks.

"Paul," he says and I curdle.

"Well Paul, I'll be back later on for that couch dance."

You have to pay for at least one couch dance. Otherwise the girls start ignoring you like a queer, or worse, cheap. This one sways from our table, skin like vinyl, muscles like a strong river current.

We're out of practice, so I lean over and remind my buddy: "Don't tell them your real name, ok?"

"That's probably good advice," Paul says.

That's when a waitress with a lazy eye approaches our table. She wants our order. Has a pen and notepad like we're at a diner.

"Bourbon. Beautiful bourbon," I holler over the din of sexual frustration. Cigarettes blaze around the darkness of the room like fire-bugs in a thicket. Mirrors refract the light onto the ceiling. The music is more annoying than the sirens of a bomb raid.

"I don't know how girls can dance to this," I say to Paul. "These hip-hop artists cut up Marvin Gaye and don't even know he was shot by his own father."

Relax, I tell myself. This is no time to get worked up. Let Paul enjoy himself. I can see he's eyeing a long-legged girl with a fuzzy black patch and rosy cheeks. She has a smile that probably makes his stomach ripple with adrenaline, deviance. He waves to her. She waves back but can't come over because she's straddling another customer.

I break his balls, jabbing him underneath the rib cage.

"I think maybe she likes you."

"You think so?"

"She likes your personality, your looks, your charm."

"Fuck you."

"Genuine love."

The bourbons arrive and I must admit I'm jazzed to be out of that dry-cleaning trap. It's been a long winter. Summer is finally upon us and I plan on getting out in my garden more often, finish what my wife started two years ago. Stupid as it sounds, I want to give back to the earth. It would make her happy.

Paul's eyes continue to wander. Abruptly, he sits up and inspects the stage. "Holy shit," he says.

"What is it?" I ask.

He nods toward the stage. "You see that retard over there in the wheelchair?"

My sight sifts through the crowd where I see, at the foot of the stage, a man in a wheelchair. The man has rumpled and magnificently twisted legs. He's enjoying himself, too, waving dollar bills around with his withered hand.

"What's he doin' here?" Paul asks.

"Evolution my friend." I slap Paul on the back. "We all need PUSSY!"

I *am* trying to change, but cheap laughs are always at hand. We pound the table and let loose, garnering the attention of the bouncers. The bouncers are big. They have chests the shape of industrial-sized propane tanks and fists like hammers.

We raise our drinks toward the wheelchaired man.

The waitress returns to our table, strutting through lewd banter and hungry hands that yearn for the touch of a female. One of her crooked eyes looks at Paul, the other one at me. Sexy in a way.

"More BOURBON!" we say and off she goes.

Paul slams his empty glass down and waves to his girl again. This time more animated, as if this garish display will free her up from the commitment of small talk with potential clients.

"COME ON OVER HERE SWEET MAMA!" he yells.

She shirks her admirer and slinks over as I tug on Paul's shirt.

"Think he's ever been laid?" I say.

Paul draws back with cold amazement. I've been doing this more and more to him lately. I ruin the night with pesky philosophical questions such as this. It's only a matter of time before he gives up on me and seeks another titty-bar cohort. That would hurt.

"You mean the retard?" he says.

I nod, but now I'm not so completely sure if the man is retarded. Maybe just crippled.

"I dunno—who'd do it with him?" Paul grabs his goatee, his charred cuticles rustling through the bristles of hair, and then answers his own question. "Maybe another retard?"

"What about a whore?"

"Doubtful."

"Why not?" I ask.

"Even a whore's got enough sense not to fuck a retard."

"What if the retard is loaded?"

Paul concedes and is about to comment but cuts the conversation short as the girl arrives and plops herself down on his crotch where he lets loose with an excited squeal.

"Am I interrupting an important conversation?" the girl asks.

"What could be more important than you?" Paul says.

"Flattery will get you everywhere, darling." The girl ruffles Paul's hair. She has blue eyes that dig into my skin like hot shrapnel. Her face is round with cheeks that remind me of the crabapples I would throw at the passing school buses as a kid.

"Name's Streeter and this here's Harris," Paul says.

A genius, my friend Streeter.

She smiles, extends her hand. "My name's Darlene."

"Nice to meet you Darlene," I say and I dig into my billfold. A quick but appreciative peek at her body and I register nipples like pink seashells. "How about giving my friend Streeter a special dance?"

I slip $50 in her g-string and give her thigh a comforting pat.

Transaction complete, she takes Paul by the hand.

"Thanks Harris," Paul says.

"No problem Streeter," I say.

Paul walks away, looks back at me, and then gestures as if the touch of her ass burns his fingers like a hot frying pan.

In the meantime, I refuse a few dance offers. One from a girl with braces and a slightly protruding belly, which would put her about two-and-a-half months pregnant. Another offer from a scag with weaves, sniffling the cocaine-tinged snot back into her nose.

Eventually, my eyes float over to the handicapped fellow near the stage. I inspect his body, his mannerisms. Soon, I'm fixated and can't stop looking.

"That's $14 for the drinks," the waitress says to me.

I slip her $20. "Keep the change," I tell her. "Come back later and give me a dance?"

My voice is tender, sincere. Two things that don't mix well in a strip joint and I think I'm as out-of-place as the retard.

"Wish I could," she says and immediately I know that's a lie. You wouldn't wish this on your worst enemy. "But the dancers tend to get bitchy when a waitress horns in on their business."

"Sit down a minute. What's your name?"

She sits, setting her tray on her bare lap.

"It's Veronica—do you need something else?"

I point to the man in the wheelchair.

"See that guy over there?"

She cranes her head toward the stage, turns back.

"You mean Marvin?"

"You know him?"

"He's a regular."

I watch his body and imagine a bug wriggling in a vice.

"I'd like to send him over a drink," I say.

She looks surprised. "Sure. He drinks Mai Tai's."

Marvin suddenly curls his head toward us like a deranged owl. He inspects us, knows we're talking about him. His face is heavy, and his eyes dance in a gelatinous pool.

"Set him up with a Mai Tai," I say.

I give Veronica the money plus a good tip. Deep down, I'm a good guy. I'm changing my ways. We then both watch Marvin as he struggles to put a bill in a girl's trapdoor. We're all into cheap thrills. Retards are no different. Men are equal.

Paul returns and plops into his seat like a spent banana peel. His eyes are droopy, laggard. It's as if God had reached down and fondled him; a hand-job from the Lord.

"That was amazing," he says.

Veronica stands, embarrassed. "I'll leave you two boys alone."

"Don't forget Marvin's drink," I say.

Veronica walks away, her pink panties reaching out through a frayed hole in her cut-off jeans.

"Who's Marvin?" Paul asks, then whirls around and winces when he sees the cripple near the stage. He turns back to me. "That drink's for the retard, ain't it?"

"Yeah," I say, defiant. "I thought the guy could use a drink."

"We all need a drink," Paul says, grabbing his bourbon/rocks, sloshing it around like some haywire cement truck.

"Here's to Marvin!" I say.

"Here's to Marvin!" Paul says.

We clink our glasses.

Soon enough Paul and I are bottomed-out drunk. I don't want to go home. I pretend I was never married. I pretend I don't work in a dry-cleaning warehouse. I pretend this night is more important than other nights. I pretend my life has disappeared.

Our friend Marvin is still at the stage with his foamy pineapple drink, eyes on the prize.

"Should we get Marvin a couch dance?" Paul's tongue is thick with bourbon.

"It'd be rude not to," I say.

"You think if we pay the girl enough," Paul says, "she might jerk him off a little bit?"

I pause and picture Marvin's rubbery member.

"I don't see why not," I say. "My girl certainly did."

Her name was Leila and she had escorted me back into the lounge area, her light pink boa fluttering along the back of her legs. A dance later and she offered her services, which surprised me.

"I didn't know this was acceptable behavior here," I said.

"It's not, but vee haff to keep up vit deez Mexican girls," Leila whispered to me. She had a Slavic grind, thin, almost fragile teeth.

I was nervous, wary of bouncers. Fumbling, Leila found my fella and grasped too brusquely. A sand-paw rub-job was not what I expected. She appeared far more delicate than her scratchy hand proved to be. Still, my stomach dropped as she slipped a condom over my stem, then the warmth of her mouth.

"What do you mean 'keep up' with the Mexican girls?"

Again with the pesky questions, I thought.

Leila stopped, wiped her mouth with the back of her hand. "Dey break de rules. Dey get all de dances vhile vee haff to scrounge around vit de odders. Vee have to keep up vit deir vays or vee go broke."

"Oh," I said, pushing her head back into position.

"We'd like to get Marvin a couch dance," Paul now tells Veronica, our waitress.

She furrows her brow, hesitates. "Marvin doesn't usually get lap dances," she says. "The stage is his thing."

"How about Leila?" I press the issue. "Is she busy?"

Veronica looks back at Leila who is sitting at a table teeming with Japanese businessmen. I watch in awe as she twirls a red drink straw between her lips. Last-call lures.

Veronica gains Leila's attention, waves her over. Leila lingers, giving the Japanese one last chance, but no takers. She flips her boa over her soft neck, saunters over.

"Bye Ryrah," says one of the Japanese men with an inebriated coo, and I think about all those lights in Tokyo, Godzilla, Gamera.

"Vat can I do for you boys?" Leila looks sharply from Paul to me. "Vant to go again?"

Veronica then takes this opportunity to disappear into the oncoming rush of lonely college boys: ball caps, tribal tattoos, shopping mall cologne, Drakkar Noir. I miss her already. Maybe I'll come up on lunch one day and ask her out.

"We're hoping you'd give our friend over there a nice dance?" Paul asks.

Leila looks at the nearly deserted stage. Suddenly, her sexiness dissipates and she slumps forward.

"Marfin?" she says, confused. "He is your friend?"

"We go way back."

"I don't know."

"Look. We just want to do something nice for the guy," I say. "We'll make it worthwhile."

Paul pulls out his wallet and I get a glimpse of the pictures of his wife, his little daughter Sandra. He tucks them neatly away without even thinking about them. He doesn't know how good he has it.

"I'm not sure about dis," she says. But then Leila reaches for the money, dejected. The bills are soggy, old.

"Leila, come here." I put my arm around her bare waist. She bends down and I whisper in her ear. "Give him the same dance you gave me."

Leila glares like she wants to punch me in the mouth.

Instead of doing so, she walks over and gives Marvin's ashen hair a rustle. She then pulls his wheelchair from its stationary position, cuts through traffic, tables and chairs. With a fading smile, she heaves and pushes the wheelchair up the back ramp to the lounge area.

The stale whiff of closing time surfaces.

"Gotta hit the pisser," Paul says. "Then we'll hit the road."

I take a final drag off my butt, smash the red-hot eye into the bottom of the ashtray. I watch Paul approach the lounge on his way back. The bouncers are at the bar, laughing. Paul stops and brushes aside the glittering beads to check up on Marvin.

I feel a warm creek of goodness trickling inside. We did a good thing. I'm helping out humanity, feeding and sheltering this poor, hungry man with an honest HJ.

Paul eventually returns. "Just saw Marvin and Leila in the lounge," he tells me. "He's scared out of his wits, man. You should've seen it."

I picture the scene in my mind—the bug struggling to get away, the skirmish to stay alive. "You think we did the right thing?" I ask.

"Go back and see how fucking happy he is."

That's when we hear a thundering CLUNK rock the entire titty establishment. Everyone looks at the back lounge. We all know what's happened. The overly eager bouncers rush over, the glimmering beads of the lounge door rattle aside. Though we know what we'll see when we get there, Paul and I rush to the action, too.

And there it is: Marvin and Leila entangled in a knot of writhing flesh, wrestling on the ground, her breasts flopping, her lingerie torn, the feathers of the boa floating in the air like a messy duck-shot. Marvin's eyes are aglow. He must've popped a fuse in his fuse-box. His pants are at his ankles. His hands locked onto Leila's fragile throat.

"Someone help her!" a fellow stripper screams.

But we don't move a muscle. We all stand and watch as Leila's face grows puffy, a mixture of blue and red bursting up through the skin. The struggle continues. The bouncers eventually surround the infuriated man—drool hanging out of his mouth like cod liver oil—and attempt to break apart his hands.

Marvin keeps his grip. Tightens it.

One of the bouncers begins slugging at Marvin's open midsection. Another bouncer evacuates the scene, extending his burly arms, moving us back with the ease of a powerful stevedore. My last glimpse is this: Leila's eyes bulging, her breath leaving her beautiful body.

Outside the club, near the curb, Paul and I are as silent as snowfall. We're standing underneath the warm glow of the neon sign, and through the closing crack of the metal door, amid all the commotion, I catch Veronica's sad eyes and sickened mouth.

She'll never concede to a date now.

I tug at Paul's shirttail to warn him of the oncoming ambulance. Local squad cars roar up behind the crowd with streaky red lights. The horns jangle my composure. Two sallow-faced paramedics move into the club with a squeaky-wheeled stretcher.

Then the metal doors slam shut again.

The crowd eventually loses interest. The fun is over. Tomorrow is now today. Some of us will go to all-night diners and stew in front of hash browns and black coffee. Some will go home to detached wives in the midst of menopause. Some will go home alone, too depressed to remove their clothes before falling face first into an empty bed.

Paul and I linger as long as we can without looking like handicapped-killing voyeurs. We watch the parking lot empty, the gravel spitting up underneath the tires. We don't speak. We hear nothing but the tinny whir of CB's from the squad cars.

"It's time to go," one of us says.

And as we stroll to Paul's car, we pass the lone handicapped space in the lot, which is occupied with a new Toyota Camry. The car has vanity license plates that say "Marvin."

Shame. Much shame.

Sailing out of the parking lot, I sink low into the passenger seat. I sink low and imagine that vice gripping the thorax of a large black beetle, the mealy, dry-apple guts pushed out and plopping to the ground, my right hand twisting the handle.

ONE MORE TRY

I feel like a Tommy-gun toting gangster heading out to the sticks to bury my girlfriend's dead cat, Norman, but dumping him in a Dumpster in the middle of Chicago is against the law (more of which I'll get to later) and I'll be damned if I pay a veterinarian to cremate and dispose of the poor beast's remains. Such a simple task doesn't deserve the services of a middleman.

To put this endeavor in a better light, part of this pet burial doesn't have much to do with money, though my father would be proud I was skirting such a bill. Being cheap is in the genes. Many stains are. More so, this is about the respect I have for Norman, and I'm actually going to regret burying him in an unmarked grave in the middle of nowhere. His way of looking at me in the middle of the night was was honest and forthright, and he deserves better, he deserves dignity.

When I first met my girlfriend Dana, Norman and I bonded in her apartment one night after his sandpaper tongue entangled my arm hair into a tight little knot. After his lickings, he retired to the warmth of my lap, his guttural purr vibrating against my loins. He fell asleep until Dana ran the can opener, leaving a sweater of tiger-striped hair in my lap, his claw marks penetrating my jeans and embedding into my thighs. Since that little get-together, I've come to like the fucker.

And let's be honest here, it'd be inhumane to drop him off at the vet like a half-defrosted turkey. The very thought of shoving Norman's furry body into an incinerator makes me feel like Hitler, or Julia Childs.

So, with a pair of plastic baggies wrapped around my hands like surgical gloves, I placed Norman into a cardboard box. I packed a shovel and a flashlight in the backseat, and I'm now on my way out to a secluded part of the woods in the middle of the night. I listen to New Orleans Funeral Jazz while the cardboard box shuffles around in the trunk like a forgotten Christmas present.

At first, Dana, who I've now lived with for three bumpy years, balked at the idea.

"You're *what*?" Dana's sadness abandoned her for befuddlement.

We were standing in the middle of our living room. The late afternoon sun had found its way through the curtains and attached itself to the back of her hair. It made the delicate strands look like burnt honey.

I have to say that Dana has this ferocious ability to make me feel everything I do is either stupid or not very-well thought out. Most of her accusations are spot-on. My batting average is low. I pay little attention to the details, and if I'm not working the night shift at the warehouse, or in the spare room studying software development, I'm usually in the process of inventing a new computer game. And I'm close. I have a winner.

"I'm going to bury Norman in the woods," I repeated to her.

I thought Dana might be more appreciative. Plus, I wanted to show her I was changing my ways. That I was taking control of my life by taking the initiative to bury this dead one, and it was an honest attempt at mending our battered relationship.

But Dana never understands my motives anymore. Her face brightened like a spotlight and her tan eyes irradiated. I was convinced she enjoyed catching me in these fits of stupidity.

"I don't think so, Steven." She said this with a tone that assumed I was joking, a tone I had come to despise. Dana is so often right she believes she's *always* right. There's never a slight chance she's mistaken. But, this time, she's wrong. Dead wrong.

Confidently, I volleyed. "I'm afraid it's the only way."

For months now, Dana and I have been going in two different directions: me to the spare room to tinker on my game, and her to her mother's house to chat about how disappointing her life has become since we've met.

I have my problems, I admit. My ways don't settle with hers. My bills are two weeks late. I never replace the toilet paper. I drive without a seatbelt. And I don't pay my parking tickets until there's a boot strangling my tire. I have to borrow money all the time. I'm not exactly reclusive, but I'm guilty for trying to live an uncomplicated, solemn life.

And Dana has become far too vicious for a man of my misgivings. In my daily bungles and snafus, I catch her sneering, her mouth curling with derision. Her favorite saying after yet another botched job: "All you have to do is *think*, Steven."

Her mother—a fine lady if a burned-out version of Sue Ellen from Dallas was your thing—doesn't help the situation. After a few high-balls, she's keen to telling Dana to find a real provider—one who contributes, one with a solid future, one who doesn't hang his hopes on mediocre cartoon animation and game development skills.

Thus, Dana and I ignore each other like we've been married for twenty-five years instead of dating for three. It's menopausal. We wake up without saying a word to one another. We eat dinner in different parts of the house. We shit with the door open. The silence swallows us both.

Nonetheless, we continue, as if our problems are downed power lines flopping around on the ground—you can only watch and hope not to get zapped as you walk briskly in the other direction.

"No fucking way!" Dana snarled back at me. "You are not taking my cat—"

"Dead cat!" I playfully interjected.

"You are not taking MY DEAD CAT and burying him in the woods! It's not right!"

"Not right?" I snorted. "I'll show you what's not right."

From my back pocket, I yanked out the burial estimates from the vet and slapped them on the table. The scrawled carbon markings made Dana's face drag. She then tucked her thick brown locks behind her ears and began whispering the numbers like she was autistic. Still, she wanted to fight a battle she was sure to lose. She definitely has spunk.

"Fuck," she said. "We don't have the money to cover this."

"Tell me about it," I said. "Now, where are the garbage bags? I need the fragrant ones, too, because he's a bit ripe."

It was good to finally be right. Victory. But that victory cost me a night of sleeplessness on a lumpy, unforgiving couch.

Norman died peacefully.

Yesterday, I found the bugger curled up stiff in the closet and nudged him with my foot. Waking Norman out of a deep sleep was a sadistic quip I indulged in every once in a while. I felt it rectified all the times he'd scratched up the furniture or puked in my shoes.

This time, though, Norman's head didn't spring up. I couldn't see the lids of his eyes curl back, or his pupils adjusting to the light. He didn't budge at all. So I crouched down and poked him with my finger where his corpse felt like a plastic doll wearing a fake mink stole.

That's when I'd stood up and backed out of the room to *think* about what should be done. The whole scene was rather disturbing, but I couldn't do anything immediate as I was late for work, so I decided to leave Norman in the closet with a note attached to the front door:

Dana,

Norman's a goner. Guess he got too old and his body quit on him. If you get home before I do, just leave him be. I'll take care of everything later. I'm really sorry, Dana. I know how much he meant to you. The weatherman said it was supposed to get up to 95 degrees today, so I hope his body doesn't begin to stink. By the way, I ate your leftover ravioli this morning.

Love you,

Steven

During my lunch break that afternoon, I paid a visit to our vet, Dr. Aki Arabaki, who is a Pakistani man with oddly stained fingers and hair growing out of his dungeon-like ears. With breath like a freshly stubbed-out cigar, he explained the options to me.

"We could cremate Norman," he suggested with a straight face, "and place his remains in a beautiful vase." Sure, I thought, and perhaps we could situate the vase on the mantel and discuss him over dinner parties? We could drink blue aperitifs and reminisce about salmon-flavored hairballs. "Or we could bury him in our pet cemetery," he continued. "We have facilities in Wheaton."

"What if I just buried him out in the backyard?"

We don't have a backyard. We don't even have a balcony or a potted fern I could stuff Norman into. Dana and I lived in a cramped apartment on the north side of Chicago. As it turns out, I couldn't bury him behind the shed next to the garden trellis even if I had one.

"No, no," the doctor said gently. "I am afraid you cannot do that."

While his tone was gentle, it was clear Dr. Arabaki was annoyed with my ignorance, and he stared at me with ice-pond eyes, his mouth purple like frozen blackberries.

"Why not?" I asked.

"The law in Chicago states that no person shall leave in or throw into any public way, public place or public theater, or offensively expose or bury within the city, the body or any part thereof of any dead or fatally sick or injured animal."

It sounded too rehearsed to be untrue. I stalled for something to say. Would Dana know if I simply tossed Norman into a Dumpster? Would the guilt stain my face? Would it ruin our chances of staying together? Like I had been told so many times before, I was trying to *think*.

"Come," Dr. Arabaki said with a wave of his hand. "Let me show you some of the lovely caskets we have on sale this month."

Respectful pet owners had proper funerals. That was for certain. For a half hour the good doctor explained all the options to me. I didn't want to insult the man, so I inhaled his quotes with a polite smile and nodded:

"Yes, yes. I understand."

"Oh, that is a very nice casket. Is that real velvet? No? It looks like real velvet!"

"Are wreaths included in this package, Dr. Arabaki?"

"What about a death certificate for bereavement? You know, for time off work? Of course, we'll have to fly in some family for the funeral."

The owner, of course, gets charged up the butt with every minor detail. One thing after another: handling fees, incinerator fees, ceremony fees, plot fees, cemetery landscaping fees, grave digger fees, death certificate taxes, taxes of all sorts. You can even have a pet mortician doll up your kitty and perch him on a funeral pyre if you were into such a thing.

But I couldn't commit. Even if every animal lover and veterinarian in the city of Chicago rallied to convince me that a cat funeral was a worthwhile event—one that would make Dana's acceptance of Norman's death a little easier—it just wasn't respectful in my eyes.

It was too serious.

Much to her consternation, Dana couldn't think of a better way to say goodbye to Norman than digging that dreaded hole in the middle of the woods. We simply didn't have money for a "proper" burial. To further my point, I opened my wallet and pulled out lint, overdrawn bank statements, and an old condom from college years.

It was an ode to yet more botched discrepancies.

Of course, Dana was too proud to hit up her mother during an afternoon of Harvey Wallbangers, and this went without saying.

"Is this charge for handling some kind of a joke?" Dana was referring to the bill again, scrunching up her sweet pink forehead.

This is when I realized our relationship was damaged beyond repair, like an arm dangling from a car window and torn from its socket by another passing car. She didn't even look to me for comfort, nor I her, and that's when I knew I really loved Dana. It was in the time of tragedy that we could truly be selfish.

"It's no joke," I said.

In consolation, I grabbed a bottle of wine from the cupboard shelf. Drinking was all I could do to show my respect, for both Norman and Dana. I poured two glasses and sat on the couch, hoping the old girl would initiate a hug-and-cuddle session. I wanted her body clinging to me like a suckerfish, thus repairing our relationship before the garbage man scooped up the remains and made a fucking nightstand out of it.

"I'll bury him out in Skokie or something tonight," I said. I didn't want to be unsympathetic. "Maybe out in Evanston, near the campus. Kids are drunk out there, they won't know what I'm doing."

"Can I go with you?"

This was the last time Dana would look into my eyes and expect an honest answer.

"That's not such a good idea Dana." I grabbed my chin in seriousness. "It's going to take me a few hours to do the deed, and I'll head out around 2:00am or so."

Norman was with Dana for fifteen years. She had kitten pictures hanging from the fridge with fruit-shaped magnets. A pineapple held up the one where Norman was taking a cool drink from the toilet; a bunch of grapes the one where he'd flipped his lid on catnip, his eyes crazed and wide; an orange the one where he was sleeping, curled up like a pill-bug.

I also didn't want our last moments together burying her dead cat. This part of the process was methodical. It's what you do with a leftover carcass. I liked Norman, but now he was refuse, chicken bones. I only wanted to help.

She began crying, but I stood my ground. "I'm sorry," I said.

I also knew that if Dana went with me she would only complain about the mosquitoes and poison ivy and the darkness of the woods. She'd want me to do everything proper under the eyes of God, too. Catholics have a way of ruining everything.

After more crying, she agreed rather half-heartedly. "Well, I do have to get up early in the morning."

I was surprised I didn't get much of a fight on that one. Perhaps she knew if she saw me burying her dead cat she'd project her pain onto me and end up despising me even more. Dana sighed through a swig of wine, and a glazed look rumbled over her like she was standing underneath a dark thunderstorm in Kansas.

"I couldn't handle seeing him anyway," she confessed. "I want to remember Norman the way he was the other day. Fat, cuddly and warm."

"That's a good idea," I said. I then drank more red and waited for 2:00am to roll around. Dana eventually fell asleep in our bed, the space between her legs empty and cold.

Animals brought us together and animals tore us apart.

Dana and I met at the circus. I know circuses aren't very romantic, what with the elephants shitting all over the place, the monkeys picking their asses, and the drunk, unhealthy clowns spitting in kids' faces. But I was there with my six-year-old nephew, Eaton. My sister's son is a good kid, smart, but always with a stomach ache. Big surprise since my sister feeds him nothing but potato chips, candy and French fries. He's a garbage disposal with legs. We get along great.

At the time, Dana was managing a concession stand at the United Center, and when Eaton barfed-up a hot dog heavy with relish and ketchup right in front of her stand, she was nice enough to help me clean it up. Not that anybody was breaking health codes with elephant dung a few hundred feet away. But I was delighted she helped because I was seconds from pretending it didn't even happen, walking away forever. I would later do the same thing whenever I found one of Norman's pink slippery piles scattered throughout the apartment.

"Is he ok?" Her voice tinkled from behind the cotton candy, which looked like giant blue and pink ear swabs.

"Yeah," I replied, startled, caught. "Little bastard eats everything he can get his hands on—you gotta watch out for your fingers!"

She was lean and had bony shoulders, with fantastic posture. I let

Dana do most of the cleaning because it seemed like the right thing to do. I watched and told her how sorry I was and patted poor Eaton's head.

I felt bad for not helping, though, and as Eaton and I walked through the tunnel and back to our seats, I caught her catching a glimpse of us both, a yearning buried deep within.

After the show, I wanted to thank Dana personally. I watched her working from afar, waiting for an open moment to catch her attention. I watched as a curl of dark brown hair slipped out of the bun on top of her head while she cleaned the appliances in back. It dangled over her left eye and mesmerized me. Pure wizardry.

"Listen," I said when she finally approached. "I want to thank you for helping me with that awful mess my nephew made earlier."

"Oh forget about it," she answered with a wave, a smile that jabbed my ribs. She didn't even think twice about cleaning up the puke. She said she was glad to help me. Dana looked into my eyes and I was lost. My stomach collapsed like an imploded building.

"Well, I just wanted you to know that I appreciate it," I told her, briefly putting a warm hand on her shoulder. It was my signature move.

"It's no problem really—at least you brought it to my attention," she said. "Most guys just walk away from a mess like that. They pretend it doesn't even happen."

"Pigs," I said.

I noticed one of her bottom teeth curled slightly inwards. It was such a wonderful flaw, and I decided to ask her to marry me someday.

My driver's side window is open and I detect the acrid smell of earthy suburbs. I roll through a lone stop sign on a barren dirt road. Here I am, on the verge of being single, thirty-one years old, not to mention broke and on my way to bury a dead, bloated cat in the middle of rural Illinois. I always thought I'd end up a bachelor, somehow, someway.

But this…

Part of me wants to shrug. Finding someone in this world—

someone that's simply worth a damn—is a ridiculous notion. Impossible in a way. But there's also part of me that will love Dana for the rest of my life. I won't forget her charming ability to belittle, or her cautionary tone while making a left-hand turn.

That's when I look up and realize my car is croaking. The alternator fails and saps the energy from my battery. The dashboard lights fade to black. It's an exquisite scene.

I pull off to the side of the road and try to kick it over, but no go.

I sit back and try to gain perspective on my life. But that engine doesn't kick over either. I'm always forgetting to replace the spark plugs, or change the oil, and give it the attention she needs and deserves. Maintenance is a bitch.

The bumpy tow ride to Pete's Garage in Skokie gives me more time to confuse the situation. The tow truck driver is a dirty grease monkey I wrangled out of the sack. Being that he's on-call, he remains reserved and sleepy. We don't say much as he drives along. I have nothing else to do but be introspective. Trace the path where Dana and I went wrong. Somewhere, she lost her generosity and nurturing attitude. Of course, I kept forgetting to buy milk, sleeping until mid-afternoon, wearing down the gasket head.

At 3:00am, the garage is closed. The tow-truck driver lowers the car, drops the hitch, and skids away into the night without a word, the dusty gravel spitting up behind him. A deep tug in my belly tells me I wanted him to stay. That maybe a chat with a complete stranger would shed light on the situation, a good old-fashioned *mano y mano*.

But his taillights squint in the darkness until they disappear and the street is empty again. There's a public telephone. Luckily, I always have change for such emergencies.

"Dana?" I whisper into the germ-infested receiver.

"Mmm? Steven? What's wrong? What did you do?"

"My car died. I'm out here in the middle of Skokie."

I hear Dana's lungs being crushed by my inability. I can see her pink lips purse in anger. I see her mottled pajamas bunched up around her legs and torso. I always wondered what the last straw would be.

"Did you bury Norman?"

"He's still in the trunk."

"Jesus, Steven."

I pause to ready her for the inevitable.

"I need some money, Dana."

I didn't mean to be so reckless, so inconsiderate. Dana should know this by now.

"Give me an hour," she says.

"Thanks," I say.

Hearing her grunt to get out of that warm bed, the mattress coils creaking, breaks me.

Dana and her drunken mother arrive just before dawn, the light blue sky washing the world clean. We stand in front of the garage and I can smell the dry vermouth on her mother's breath as they begin to spit advice at me.

In so many words, they tell me I'm wrong for this world. They tell me I need to *think* before acting. And after sleeping on a bench half the night, the unrelenting chirp of crickets grating their legs, I wasn't in the mood for such lectures.

"Are you even *listening* to us, Steven?" Dana asks, her brow crinkled with exasperation.

I stay silent, which is another mistake.

"Do you see what I mean?" I hear her mother whisper to Dana.

"Oh mom!"

In the midst of their squawking, I take a walk to clear my mind.

"Steven! Wait!"

Dana catches up in the parking lot, tugs at my elbow. Her face says it all. Her face says, *I know this is tough, but this is your fault.*

"I can't explain myself anymore, Dana," I say. "I'm tired of it."

"I know. I know." She's still holding my elbow. Her soft touch melts me. I wish it were an act of reconciliation. But these caresses are an act of mercy. "Just ignore her."

"It's not her I'm worried about," I say.

We eventually walk back to her mother's car side by side, a million miles apart. I crawl into the backseat and stare out the window at the desolate fields and barren streets.

We don't wait for the mechanics. Too many witnesses.

With Norman successfully transferred to the depths of her trunk, Dana's mother sets course for our broken apartment. I can see—over a pot of sobering coffee and a much-too serious talk at the kitchen table—our indefinite separation lingering in the foreground.

In the rearview mirror, the old bag smirks at me, her eyes a slurry of drunken red.

"Happy hour finally catching up with you Mrs. Devalano?" I ask from the backseat.

Dana turns and glares. This is the first time I've ever taken a crack at her mother. It doesn't feel as good as I thought it would. Foreign.

"I'm just fine Steven," Dana's mother says. After another moment, she looks again into the rearview mirror and winks. "I'm just worried about you is all. Failure at yet another simple task."

The old bag continues to drive with a newfound zest while Dana slumps back into the passenger seat, a scowl darkening her beautiful face, the radio alive but the sound just above a burble.

Four days later, Dana has a proper funeral for Norman.

I was sent an invitation out of something less than respect. The card has a drawing of a tiger-stripped cat on a cloud. There's also a shining harp in the background, wings. Cat heaven.

Dana's mother foots the bill for the event.

I've already moved my belongings to a storage facility on the west side. I'm temporarily staying on a friend's couch, which stinks like a mangy dog. The dog, Carlos, died three years ago, but his robust stink lingers like a legend.

The funeral proceedings are murder. Dana's mother squints at me the entire time, her moral superiority settling into my bones like cancer. Her father, however, to whom I now owe $500 for a new alternator, ignores me and stares into the sky with mild annoyance.

Dana sits in between the two. Beaten, ragged, but relieved this whole ordeal has finally come to a close.

Norman looks the happiest. It's an open casket. I bought a wreath. And as I lean in and pay my last respects, I see contentment pasted across his face. He's happy that his body is finally going to the earth where it belongs. His spirit now has a home, and for that, I'm grateful.

The service is standard fare. There's a eulogy about a better place, nine lives, all that hogwash. Again, like the garage out in Skokie, Dana catches up with me in the parking lot, and I overcome the urge to stay quiet, or revert to old excuses.

"It was bound to happen," I assure her. "I'm a fuck-up."

"Don't say that." She scowls. "It's just that—"

"I know what it is Dana. We both do."

I'll miss her sweeping up after breaking a dish or knocking over the garbage can filled with soiled cat litter.

"So where's the wake?" I say.

Sometimes you think it never hurts to joke.

Sometimes you are wrong.

"Thanks for trying, Steven." Dana takes my elbow again and I feel like embracing her warm body, but that would only deprive me of future inadequacies. "I know you were doing what you thought was right."

I've heard somewhere that failure makes your next attempt even stronger. But failure puts me on a piss-drizzled couch, girlfriend-less. In a way, maybe it's good advice. I'll try to move on. I'll try to make someone else a little happier than she.

"I'll pay your old man for the alternator as soon as I can."

Dana looks into my eyes. She doesn't expect honesty anymore, which is good because I wasn't giving her any. I'm more broke than when I began this ordeal, and I planned on stiffing her father from jump street.

"My father says to forget about the money."

Smart girl. She's severing our connections for good. She won't be the hamster for my new computer game, which is now on hold due to a lack of funding. Her harsh stance lessened, her eagerness to jump down my throat by the wayside, Dana smiles one last time for me, her gnarled tooth capturing my love once again.

"Take care of yourself, Dana."

"You too, Steven."

She leans in and kisses my cheek lightly. The candy-flavored scent of her perfume dances into my nostrils. Dana then walks away forever. I can already picture her in our apartment, on the couch with a boyfriend less unstudied and with no social impediments, very stable. It'll be an incredibly rewarding relationship. The poor girl.

The good news is she'll have a new cat with Golden Fleece and ears that will twitch when you call him by his name: Norman II, the second coming.

ERWIN'S MAIN ATTRACTION

When my wife Claire bursts through the front door and tells me she's going to be one of the new tour guides on Danny Tipton's latest and greatest roadside attractions, "Appalachia's Haunted Trailways," I'm concerned but not surprised.

Erwin is that kind of town.

"Red!!" she screams, the storm door clacking shut, the stony smell of summer-warmed pavement right behind her. Claire stands tall as a beanstalk, and round in all the right places. She's panting, jumping up and down, her forearms pressing into her wonderful bosoms. Most nights, I can't get a word edgewise. Today is no different. Girl is already in mid-story. "Danny Tipton's openin' a new business! Guess who's gonna run it?"

Claire approaches as if to give our after-work embrace, a ritual we've had for fifteen years. It's what keeps us close. She starts shaking my shoulders instead, hastening my answer. "Come on, Red!"

I tell you, she's wired.

"Glory Boy?"

Claire frowns.

To me, this passes as funny. I mean no harm, and if it sounds cruel it's because Glory Boy is the deaf-mute fella who lives across the crick here. Poor kid lost his hearing surviving the worst bout of spinal meningitis the state of Tennessee ever seen.

That's why we call him Glory Boy.

That year the entire town prayed for GB. We staged vigils, fundraisers, hot dog eating contests. He was the focus of our lives.

The news made daily reports. Journalists glorified him. Kid now works at WalMarts in town, and does a damn fine job of stocking those shelves, too. But, like I said, I joke around to lighten the mood.

My wife forgives me most of the time.

"No! It's me! It's *me*!"

Claire forces herself into my arms and I give the girl a loving squeeze, a few pats on the behind. "Congratulations, babe," I say into her ear, the scent of burning ozone in her hair. Claire uses a half can of hairspray a day. The old aerosol cans. Super hold.

We push into the kitchen for dinner.

"I'm really proud of you," I say.

Claire cracks a smile from ear to ear. She grabs a skillet and the blue flames of the stove hiss.

At first, my statement holds true: I *am* proud of her. Her job means more security and it'll get her out of the house, too.

"This is gonna be so great!"

Of course, I have my doubts. She's worked with Danny Tipton before, many moons ago, and I'll be damned if I wasn't gonna chime in with my two cents. "You know," I say, hands on my hips. "I just don't care for Danny Tipton. He's not a sensible man."

I didn't want to burst Claire's bubble. She's been after a job for over a year now, applying everywhere: The Washing Well, Erwin's local laundry mat; the receptionist for Johnny's Big Toe, a towing service in Burnsville. She even begged to be the shoe-cleaning girl at Big Mary's Bowl-A-Rama, spraying disinfectant into everyone's dirty rentals.

No one's hired her.

Also, this isn't Danny's first foray into entrepreneurship. The last was a fledgling whitewater rafting tour, the warehouse of which mysteriously burned down in the middle of a warm summer night four years ago. Morning after the fire, you could see the black clouds of smoldering rubber rafts from miles away. It was never proved as arson, but everyone knew the incident to be a bit hinky.

Things steadily got worse for Danny. After collecting the insurance money, his secretary, Ann Filmore, one of Claire's best friends, turned up pregnant (with Danny's seed, of course) and was soon seeking out the Spruce Pine abortionist. Later that fall, a shitload of lawsuits cropped up from the neck injuries a few rafters suffered while rafting the low waters of the Nolichucky.

That's when Danny disappeared. Nobody knew where. Nobody knew how. We only recently found out he was back in Erwin after spending some quality rehab time in the Yancey County Mental Health and Nursing Center.

Despite all the unwritten womanly codes, I knew my wife would be quick to defend Danny. I could see the explanation sitting on her tongue, squirming in her mouth like a night crawler approaching a fishing hook.

"You're worried about Danny Tipton?" Claire waves me off with her blue-veined hand. "He's harmless!"

"That might've been true when he was in a padded room with veins full of lithium."

"I can take care of myself, Red."

Watching Claire maneuver the skillet, I pay attention to her facial tics. I can spot her tells, feel them in my bones. Claire notices my needling and says, "He's fine! They wouldn't have let him out of that hospital if he weren't right. Right?"

"If you say so."

"We all deserve second chances, don't we?"

"I believe we do."

I still didn't like the situation.

I also didn't like the role Claire played in Ann Filmore's subsequent vacuuming, either. My wife plagued the town with absurd stories and lies about the two, an attempt to lead the hounds of Erwin astray from a perfectly good scandal. I know she did it out of care, to protect Ann. I've never had much reason to doubt my wife, and I didn't feel good about starting right then and there. Claire's a good bird, a rightly Christian woman.

She fumes a bit now but carries on with dinner, slapping down a mound of raw red hamburger into the pan, tossing the packaging into the garbage, grabbing a spatula. Claire is an attractive lady. She always a milky glow behind her long neck. Her cheeks dimpled and red like the candied cherries in a fruitcake. It can be distracting.

I say to her, "Well? Ain'tcha gonna tell me all about it?"

This sets Claire's mouth a runnin'. She tells me how she ran into Danny at the Bi-Lo, how healthy he looked, how he'd bought that haunted land over near the Asheville Highway, the ghosts, the goblins, the folklore of the Appalachians.

"Danny bought the old Laws' house. He says there's hauntings out there every dern night!"

I've heard plenty about the ghosts of the Appalachians, but I never bought into them. My aunt Catherine would tell me stories: mysterious and well-dressed men floating in caskets, haunting the city's Municipal Building, blood-curdling screams from the banks of the Toe River, ghastly specters dancing in and out of the train tunnels. They were scary enough as a kid. My aunt believed in her stories. She sold them. But I grew up and became skeptical. Hairy, too.

"This is so exciting." Claire manipulates the browning flesh, the hamburger mixing with the helper. "I didn't know those trails were haunted, did you?"

I grab a glass of sun-brewed from the fridge, feel the cool rush of mechanized breath from the fan, the stale tang of old mustard.

"Whole region is haunted, if you believe in that sort of thing."

Claire's shoulders deflate as I come up from behind, tea in hand. I smooch her ear, cup a breast, the right one. I like that one best. She shrugs me off, though I don't know whether she's irritated with my advances or my doubting.

"Sorry, hon." I let go. "Happy you're working is all. Tell me more."

I then sit at the kitchen table, my arm-skin sticking to the Okracoke plastic mats. I open up the newspaper, dive into the obits and worry about what Danny Tipton's got cooking.

That night we turn in early. No lovemaking, no fooling around. Claire wants to rest. Tomorrow is her big day, and she doesn't want to spoil it by getting comfortable and sleeping in late. She keeps fidgeting in bed, scratching, swallowing hard.

"Red?"

I open my eyes and see dark whorls.

"Danny's a changed man."

"I believe you."

"He's got great ideas for the tour."

"That right?"

There's a fall of silence, some bunching up of covers.

"You really proud of me?"

I flip over, snuggle in, and kiss her smooth cheek.

"Of course I am."

I can see why she has her doubts.

Since we've wed, Claire's never held a gig for more than a few months. It doesn't bother me. I'd rather have my wife home watching QVC and fighting her compulsive urge to order angelic trinkets than working a dead-end job for some yo-yo like Danny Tipton.

Claire's simply had a string of bad luck lately. She's been fired, laid off, suspended, downsized, ousted, and transferred. She just quit her most recent gig peddling that tourist garbage down at The Heritage Museum, located smack-dab in the middle of town.

Of all the two-bit jobs, Claire liked that one most. In the end, the owner accused her of dealing Girl Scout cookies on the side. Our cousin's daughter, Sue Ellen, couldn't get rid of her pre-bought stash, so Claire pushed them off on the tourists. My wife means well, likes to do the right thing, though the right thing would've been telling Sue Ellen to get off her prissy little ass and hustle the supermarkets. Those cookies pretty much sell themselves.

There was a minor scuffle with the owner, a hospital visit, and the whole fiasco ended with a suspended merchant's license. This happens a lot to Claire. She gets mixed up in moral dilemmas, torments her conscience, and ends up in the middle of lawsuits.

Prior to that, my wife would come home from the Museum with a big smile and tell me all about the tourists that'd come in and buy that garbage. "You should have seen it." She'd have eyes bright as bonfires. "This family of Indians came into the store today!"

"Dots or feathers?"

"Dots or feath?—they're called bindi's, Red! Listen, they cleaned the place out. They bought ten of everything! Shirts, mugs, key chains, shot glasses. The works!"

"Kind of shots you think they shoot in India?"

"You don't get it, do you? They cleaned us out!" Claire was proud when the store had a good day, like it put Erwin on the map of the world.

"Ask me, that tourist propaganda just perpetuates those awful rumors about Erwin."

She'd wave me off. "You make too much of it."

This is probably true. But the major sellers at the museum are any one of the numerous gifts with Big Mary printed on the front of it. If you don't know, and I'm sure most of you don't, Big Mary was the circus elephant that was publicly executed here in Erwin back in 1916. They hung her from a railroad crane.

Not much of a punch line to follow that statement, and most of the prideful folk 'round these parts can be a bit testy when referring to Erwin's sordid history, believe me.

Over the years, we Erwinians have taken all the teasing we can handle. We dislike the gleeful tourists who descend upon our small town to pester us about Mary's burial ground, her remains, her legend. Even our pastor turns his nose at the nicest of strangers who gather 'round the town fountain like a pack of squabbling ducks, the kids donning t-shirts with a picture of an elephant strung up by an industrial metal chain.

Most of 'em are northerners. We have nothing against northerners, particularly, but they can be persistent and nosy and will often wander the streets and stare at us like we're circus hands or sideshow freaks. Sometimes they end up over near the rail yard on the other side of town, ogling the railroad cranes.

"Get away from there!" Charlie Boat will growl at them.

Charlie, the only black man in Erwin—though there are two Hispanic families now and a Chinese restaurant with *real* Chinese hosts—works security at the rail yard and has to shoo the tourists away like hungry rodents. He'll catch me at Shirley's Diner and complain 'til his black face turns purple.

"Bastards were at it again today, Red!" He'll slap the table, his grits going cold. "I keep telling 'em: 'Those ain't the cranes Big Mary was hanged with!' No sir! These cranes today couldn't stand the girth of that dad-gum elephant, Red! Crazy fools!"

Much as some of us would like to mask this execution, the city of Erwin revolves around it. Our forefathers, the people who built this town—engineers, statesmen, professors—made the sober decision to hang the poor girl after she went on a rampage and killed three innocent bystanders at the circus that summer afternoon.

My guess is the townsfolk wanted to make a statement.

The incident stains me particularly. My grandfather hoisted the crane that killed the beast. My father told me the story when I was old enough, and afterwards I had horrible dreams about that elephant, dangling, limp and lifeless, the scuffed gray skin around her eyes. There are newspaper clippings on the wall at The Heritage. At the bottom, below an austere looking gentleman, next to the bloated elephant, it reads:

Mr. John LeClaire, crane operator. My grandfather.

Unfortunately, Erwin is a poor town. We depend on the nuclear plant and pottery industry to get us by, so the extra income from the tourists proves handy to most, even if that means hocking coffee mugs that depict our darkest hours as a city.

But my concern ain't Claire playing this small role in screwing the city yokels out of their hard-earned cash. Hell, one scam is as good as another, and all sorts of abandoned mines have cropped-up the past few years, fobbing themselves off as "genuine" gem searches. She could easily work there. With savvy advertisements, any local murder can be converted into a profitable tourist attraction. Around these parts, tragic mining accidents become legends and then become carnival rides.

There's an entire industry that thrives on Erwin's lies.

No, I'm more concerned about Claire's tightening relationship with Danny Tipton, who's become a local celebrity here in Erwin since his return.

In the morning, I slug into the kitchen wearing polar bear slippers and Claire's pink silk robe, my face in need of a sharp razor. The robe is open, revealing my burly chest and anchor tattoo etched into my skin when I was in the Navy.

"Couldn't sleep?" I ask.

"Not a wink."

My wife dishes out the vittles. Her eyes are puffy and aggravated and she's adjusting to the sun, which is spreading across the room from the sliding glass door. I take pride in cleaning that glass door, though I hate to see the sparrows and finches smack into it on occasion.

"Time you have to be in?" I ask.

Claire dumps the hot skillet into the sink with a sizzle and looks at the clock on the stove. It's 7:52. "Danny wants us there at 8:00 for training." She gulps at some coffee, emits a cute, burning burp.

"Who are the other trainees?"

I pour a thin drool of syrup over my French toast.

"Claire?"

"What?"

"I said 'Who are the other trainees?'"

"There's only two of us."

"Well, who is the other one?"

"You know Pam Dawson?"

"Wasn't she prom queen a year ago?"

"Think so."

"Little young to be working. Shouldn't she be off at college?"

"I don't know. I gotta run, Red."

My wife gives me a kiss on the cheek, her perfume sweeping by like a bus wreck. I knife up some toast, listening to her tires grind through the gravel driveway.

Claire is late for everything, even her own Tupperware parties, which she hosts every few months. With each passing year we acquire more salad spinners and colanders and spaghetti strainers than you can imagine. Our cupboards are bulging. Everything we own is sealed up in dishwasher-safe containers: corn flakes, laundry detergent, miscellaneous hardware and coupons, even tampons and other toiletries.

Myself, I'm always on time. Root canals, prostate exams, driver's license registration, and especially work. I work at Erwin's National Fish Hatchery, which is north of Harris Hollow Road. I've been there for ten years and I've never been late. I like my job. Everyday it's a silvery collage of rainbow trout and agriculturists. They're a bickering bunch—the agriculturalists, not the brood fish.

I'm the head grounds keeper. I punch in at 9:00am everyday and then head out to the pump house for my daily routine. With various forms of maintenance, my day consists of keeping the raceways clean and ensuring that the ponds and tanks are well below 65 degrees.

My favorite part of the job is feeding the trout. At noon, I shovel the pellets into the water with little 'ploops' and watch their bodies writhe and flap, and it makes me feel I'm doing my part in life's weird circle. I'm a crucial link to evolution, the advancement of their species. Fishing has always been one of America's leading forms of outdoor recreation.

Driving to town in my work vehicle is usually a calming experience. We live on the western outskirts of Erwin and the area is a stunning place to live. Large eastern hemlocks loom at the lower basins of the valley. Splotches of red spruce at the higher elevations. Bald patches of mountain sticking out at the tops like smooth eggs.

But this morning I don't enjoy the drive at all. The clean air, the trees, nothing diverts me from Danny Tipton and Pam Dawson. She's so young, so pretty, and so vulnerable I'm afraid Danny'll impregnate her like he did Ann Filmore. Last I heard, Ann'd packed her bags and beat feet for Charlotte. They say she works downtown as a meter maid, putting orange tickets onto illegally parked cars. That's no life to live.

Claire, I'm not so worried about. She's a tough girl. One night, I watched her kick Randy Soda in his balls after his hand "accidentally" brushed up against her apple-shaped bottom. This was at The Bee's Hive. I watched it happen from across the bar. She kicked, he went blue in the face, doubled over and went down like a sack of taters. Randy Soda might not be the toughest guy in town, but he ain't no slouch, either.

As I get to work and feed the trout, I imagine Danny's hands squirming all over Pam's body like a slimy octopus, chasing her around his office, her skirt and tight blouse causing his brain to short circuit. He's got no self-control. My wife would tell me stories when she filled-in a couple days at his whitewater outfit, shortly before it was bar-b-qued.

"You should see those two, Red," she would say after coming home at night, slipping into a nightgown, her breasts reacting to the touch of silk. Claire's always happy and sexual when employed. "Danny forces himself on Ann all day long."

"That right?" I'd say, patting the bedsprings.

"She pretends it bothers her, but I know she enjoys it."

No one parted on good terms. Especially after both girls attacked Danny in the library parking lot when he refused to help with Ann's abortion. Claire socked him in the puss and Ann gave him a fleshy knot on the brow with her high-heeled snakeskins.

Claire came home after the attack and asked, "Can't we just let Ann borrow the money, Red?" Like she was exasperated from whippin' Danny's hind end.

I was glad to help. I put on a troubled look and signed my Christian name at the bottom of the check, feeling like a hero. Then the fire burned down the warehouse, Danny disappeared, Ann did, too, and all was mostly forgotten. That is, until Danny popped back up again.

Along the Asheville Highway, I follow signs pointing me to "The ONLY Haunted Trailway in the Appalachian Mountains." Which is complete horsepucky. Just last summer I saw some tourist haunts along the southern end of the Blue Ridge Parkway, down near Mt. Pisgah. Creepy statues, cobwebs, blood on the fences. The whole bit.

I pull onto an old dirt road that leads to the old Laws' property, the branches of the trees scraping the top of my SUV. At the end of the holler, I see an old barn with Claire's Subaru parked in front. No other cars around. No signs of life. The trees are quiet, the ground still.

I shut down the engine and sit in the driveway. Everybody must be at lunch, or getting office stationary. Most likely they're at Shirley's Diner. Claire takes forever searching the menu and then orders the Denver omelet every time. Morning, noon, and night. Says it makes her think of Denver, though she's never been west of St. Louis.

I can only imagine what Danny's doing to get into Pam's pants. Being cute and flirtatious and offering her a raise on the first day. Playing footsy underneath the table. Ordering for her, paying for lunch, and leaving a big fat tip. It burns me up.

The barn is a mess and needs to be renovated. Broken slats, rusty hinges, a sagging middle. Over the entrance, scrawled in white paint: "Appalachian's Haunted Trailways" with badly painted ghosts and goblins on either side of the title, a witch riding a broomstick, her hairpins falling to the ground.

I don't believe in ghouls or vampires or hillbilly zombies or the supernatural, but the place gives me the willies.

"Red!" says a raspy voice from my driver's side blind spot.

I jump out of my skin, instinctively reaching for the keys in the ignition, ready to flee. I turn and see who it is and say, "Jesus, Danny. I didn't hear you come up."

Danny snickers through a newly grown moustache. He appears older. His eyes stable, his hair gray and stately. "Don't soil yer drawers, Red. I was working out yonder and heard your car pull up."

I look behind him and ask, "Where're the girls at?"

Danny looks down at the dirt like he ate the last piece of rhubarb pie. I wonder if he feels remorse for what he did to Ann. I'd hate to have Claire mixed up in any more scandals.

"Went to town for lunch." Danny then sweeps his arm toward his land. "Way too much to do here to bother."

I look again at the mess. "I see that."

I let my grip go, an imprint of my house key in my palm.

"Nice digs." My heart eventually rises from the folds of my stomach. "How many acres?"

"Deed says twenty-five." Danny spits, gripping his hands. "But I reckon maybe thirty. Can't really tell without a property fence on top 'a that hill there."

Through the windshield, I look up to the summit. The long wisps of dry, colorless grass swaying in the summer breeze.

"She flat on top?" I exit my vehicle, the ground mucky and soft. Danny's thinner than I remember, gangly. "You look good."

"Been a coon's age since I last seen you, Red."

We shake hands and square up.

"You fixin' to put a house up there? Or a trailer?"

"God no! Makes you think I'd want to do that?"

"Seems like a perfectly good place for it is all."

Danny juts his head forward. I think 'taken aback' is the term most folks use.

"Don't you know anything 'bout this place, Red?"

"What? You don't seriously believe in—"

He crosses his arms over his chest. "I believe every word about this area. Even my Mamaw warned me about buying this place. She says Terry Laws was beaten to death by his brother in a cave right down the path there. He comes out and haunts every night!"

Danny points back behind the barn. I feel my forehead scrunch. "Seen 'em with my own eyes, too."

"Seen what?" I ask.

Danny beckons me toward the barn. Over his shoulder, he says with a hearty laugh, "Stay out here past midnight sometime, Red, and you'll see *everything*."

Just like a car salesman; vague, but fully invested, luring me. I admit, though, he's got me thinking. Danny believes. That alone should get tourists to pay full price.

Inside the barn is dark, cool. The place smells of soft wood and wet hay, animal dander. There's a golf cart in the corner, on its last legs. The upholstery is worn, the split leather exposing sponge the color of barfed-up pumpkin.

"Hop on, I'll take you for a tour."

"Naw. I gotta get back to work soon, Danny."

"Come on! Won't take but a few minutes!" He cups his mouth, whispers, "It's a freebie!"

I don't really want to, but I am curious. Perhaps there are ghosts out there? Perhaps there's a reason to trust Danny Tipton? "Free, huh? Well, why didn't you say so?"

Danny starts the cart with a wheeze and we head back into the sunshine, the path muddy from the recent rain. "Gotta get me a jeep. These paths go all the way back, but this cart won't make it. There's interesting scenery out near the river. It was used for Civil War graves."

The cart tops out at 15MPH, but Danny takes the corners full blast. We dodge oncoming branches while he narrates. "See that tree stump there? That's where Minnie Riley buried her husband, Roy. Beat the poor son of bitch to death with a frying pan. She tried to cover him up before anybody took notice."

This I've never heard. The rest of the Riley's, as far as I knew, were nice people. Horse breeders, cake bakers, Erwin preservationists.

"Why'd she go and do that?"

"Mamaw says Roy was cheatin' on her with a youngin'. Guess he taught high school over near Jack's Creek and got caught with his pants down." Danny grins, his teeth sharper than a mink's. I can't tell if his smile is because of his inside information or something else.

"Been pickin' Mamaw's brain lately, eh?"

"She knows everything 'bout Erwin. She says family feuds 'round these parts always lead to black eyes or missing limbs or even cold-blooded murder."

Another hairpin turn.

It seems Danny has only wholesome ideas about his new business. Maybe Claire and Pam are not only safe, but can even benefit from the experience. Danny's changed, flipped his lid, turned a new leaf. Maybe he needs a partner in this claim? Claire's always wanted to run her own business, and we have plenty in the bank to invest in such a scam.

We pass a cluster of trees, the branches like ashy bones, the roots creeping out of the soil. The cart halts. "Couple of Civil War soldiers buried near these trees," Danny says. "Confederates turned blue coat. 'Battle of Red Banks' is what they called the skirmish, though you won't find that in your history books."

"That right?"

"I haven't seen much from these soldiers, but I hear horses trampling on occasion. Voices, too."

We try silence. I'm amazed at Danny's knowledge, his acumen. He's done his homework. I watch him strain to hear something.

"Nothing today either," he whispers.

Danny starts the golf cart, puts her back into gear and we haul off back towards the barn. The land is old but beautiful and reeks of violence and dismemberment. At every corner there's a landmark that bears a stain of death.

"Gonna charge twenty bucks per tour," he yells over the snapping of branches. "We'll start before twilight each night. The whole trip will be narrated by me or someone who's qualified."

Maybe he'll train Claire right away? It's a sure move up in pay scale. Claire's wise to these stories of the South, and she's a talker, too, full of charm. I could help her prepare each night as we dive into the sheets.

"Afterwards, there'll be refreshments and drinks and everybody'll get a discount on the books we'll sell in the barn."

"Like the ones from The Heritage Museum?"

"Exactly," he says.

There's a whole series at the museum on the haunted sights of the South. The more Danny talks, the more I'm sure he'll clean up on profits. I can see it around Halloween: a quaint setting in the barn, banana bread, cider, ghost music in the background, maybe homemade wine from the vines I saw back there. People will love it.

I slap him on the back. "You have this tourist thing by the balls."

Danny's all smiles. "We haven't made a cent yet."

"Not yet. But you seem to be enjoying it—I'm glad for ya."

"Thanks, Red. I am enjoying it."

Danny cuts hard and splashes another puddle, the muddy spray covering the path like brownie batter. "My research on Erwin and these mountains has been a good way to get healthy, too." He turns to me. "I've changed, Red. I mean it. I wanted to learn more about where we've come from and where we've been as a community."

Danny's about to shed a tear, like he's fighting for his life. I'm just not sure if he's trying to convince me or himself.

"Not sure what they did to you in that rehab center, Danny," I say as he blushes. "But you seem to be a new lad."

Danny wells up and I thump his back, a manly gesture I learned from my father. The old man would tap me in the hollow of my back with the butt-end of his wrist whenever I struck out in baseball or broke the neighbor's kitchen window with a wrist-rocket or killed a cat when I didn't mean to.

"Think the girls are back at the barn yet?"

"Don't know." Danny sniffles.

"Let's go see, shall we?"

We zip off down the path.

Back at the barn, Danny is all hospitality, a convincing business-man. It's hard not to trust him. I feel he's changed. Claire's right, I need to give people a second chance. On my way over, I had plans to thrash this man, drown him off the ruddy banks of the Toe.

Danny hands me a cassette tape. "That's a narration of the tour. I could use some feedback." Though it sounds like 'feedbag.' "It's a rough version. Still getting the nooks and crannies worked out. We'll put it to DVD and offer it as a companion to the narrated tour."

He's got the right idea, all the angles covered.

"The internet?" I ask. "A website?"

He clicks his tongue, points at me with his forefinger. "Got one of my guys workin' on that now." Danny shuffles behind a foldout table and pulls a shirt from a dog-eared cardboard box. He holds it to his chest. The shirt is orange and has black writing, two crudely designed ghosts near the nipple-areas. "Appalachian's Haunted Trailways."

"You look like an extra large." He tosses me the shirt. It smells like fresh plastic, detergent. We then head toward my vehicle.

"I'm lookin' forward to seeing the finished product, Danny. Think I can get another freebie?"

"Be my pleasure, Red."

I open the door to my SUV, the official sticker for Erwin's National Fish Hatchery peeling at the edges, the white dying to bad-meat brown.

"Let me know what you think of that tape." I raise the tape like we're toasting a drink on New Year's Eve. "Perhaps I forgot something or something your folks could add."

"I sure as shit don't have anything, but my aunt Catherine'd whip up some stories if she were still alive."

"It's all folklore 'round here, Red." He looks at me like a teacher. "It's what you choose to believe in is what matters."

We say our goodbyes and I put the car in drive.

As I head down the dirt road, further away from the holler, I see a car driving at me like a bat out of Hades. It's a black Buick, firing on all cylinders. The path is only big enough for one car, and I barely have enough time to stop.

We almost crash head on, my tires skidding, the dust furling on all sides of the vehicle. I pull next to the Buick's driver side window and sense urgency. I stick out my hand and give the international sign for 'Roll down your goddamned window!'

It's Frank Dawson and his daughter Pam in the front seat. Pam's got mascara smudged around her eyes like a raccoon. Frank's face is red as a beet. Dawson and I went to Erwin High School together. He excelled in sports: wrestling, pole vaulting, archery.

"Where's the fire, Frank?" I see that Claire is in the backseat with her hands between her legs, her crow-black eyes darting like she's watching two squirrels run amok.

"Outta the way, Red," Franks yells. "This is doesn't concern you."

Of the years I've known Frank, he's never been so determined, so angry or gruff. Not even when he was firing bows through stacks of hay with bull's-eyes, snagging state championship banners and traveling the country to display his accuracy.

"Now wait a minute."

"This doesn't concern you, Red!"

"The hell it don't," I shout back. "My wife is in the backseat of your car, Frank."

Seeing enough room to pass, Frank Dawson does so, rough-ing the sides of his car through the brush, clipping my fender. I put my vehicle in reverse and follow, the orange shirt in the backseat more fra-grant with each passing yard.

By the time I get to the driveway, where I'd parked a few minutes ago, talking to Danny, Frank is already out of the car. Claire is, too. Pam stays put in the Buick.

"Claire?" I sling the car door shut. "What the hell's going on?"

Before I get the story, both Claire and Frank take off after Danny Tipton, who's hightailing away on his golf cart, splashing through the muck. Danny has one of his new orange shirts on. Frank has steel in his right hand. I'm sure it's loaded.

"Claire! Get back here!"

She turns, a glum crinkle across her forehead. Frank, with sand-colored camouflage pants and army boots, continues down the path.

"Oh Jesus Christ!" My wife is frantic. Her legs wobbling, lips a twitter. Her face looks like her face before she pukes. "He's gonna kill Danny!" Claire dives into the heat of my chest.

"What happened?" I squeeze hard.

Claire moans, beats my chest like she's Jane and I'm Tarzan. She pulls away and points to Pam in the car. "He took Pam out into the woods. He tried to…"

I shake my wife, rattling sense into her.

"What? He tried to what?"

"He tried to rape her, Red! Don't you get it? Danny's sick!"

There's relief, almost joy.

I look over and see Pam buried in shame. Her jaw muscles tight-en. There's an abundance of resentment lurking in her tiny body, deep down. She hates us, hates the world. She's embarrassed and fraught, and has no damn reason to be. She didn't do anything wrong.

"Are you sure? There's no mistake about it?"

Claire looks at me, wide-eyed. "Who are you going to believe, Red?!? Me or him?"

"What do you mean?"

"Danny tried to rape her!"

I feel the ghosts of the Appalachian's coming out to haunt. They're telling us we deserve our misfortune, that we deserve worse. I see Danny's ideas burning up in smoke; the warehouse, the shirts, the rubber rafts. His golf cart abandoned and sinking into the river.

"You don't believe me?"

I stay silent and wonder if my wife and Pam haven't concocted this whole mess from the very beginning. Did she set Danny Tipton up? Is this revenge for Ann Filmore?

"I—"

"You what?"

I look into my wife's eyes and see those trembling saucers of milk around her dark but forgiving pupils. I want to believe her. I want to be confident.

"Red?!"

"Of course I believe you."

It's a statement I'm not so sure is true.

Then we hear the gun blast twice. Because he's such a marksmen, I'm certain Frank hit his target. He's a dead-eye. Claire stiffens, yelps like a branded goose, and collapses into my arms. I hold her tight.

From inside the Buick, I hear stifled sobs. I hear years of therapy.

I rock my wife to near-sleep.

"Should we call the police?" Claire asks after the reign of silence, the summer breeze going stale. I brush the hair from her eyes, kiss her salty forehead. She's beautiful, my wife. I've told you that before.

"Let's go."

We then head to my work vehicle and call Erwin's Police Station. I know the number by heart. I punch the keypad, my entrails feeling like they passed molten lava.

"Hey Chief?" I say.

"Red?" The warmth of cellular waves hit my ear and I give the chief the story.

The chief's name is Ned Byers. We have drinks and play billiards at The Wet Hen sometimes. We play for money and I'll kid him he's doing something illegal, that someone should slap the cuffs on him and haul him off to jail. He just laughs, sinks the eight ball and collects the kitty on the table near our beers. Real nice fella.

Anyway, Ned'll be the one to come down and make us fill out those silly reports. He'll be the one to call the coroner. He'll be the one to put Frank Dawson in cuffs.

What I'm not sure about is who'll be responsible for Danny's story. The tabloids and papers will get it wrong. Eventually, he'll be buried atop Red Hill with the rest of the Tipton's.

Perhaps his Mamaw will tell his tale over and over again 'til it becomes legend, folklore. Perhaps even Danny Tipton will be responsible for the Danny Tipton story? Perhaps he'll haunt this area for a long time to come?

Then again, I'm not so sure about that, either.

LOSING FOCUS

In the hospital room, right after the doctors tell my father the surgery has successfully removed all the cancer inside his testicles, he kisses my mother, looks deep into her scared green eyes and says, "Things are going to change around here."

And change they do.

My father stops coming home directly after work. Instead, he drives around half the night with a six-pack of tall boys in his lap and cruises his old neighborhood in the Clark Park section of Detroit. He clings to the past, dissolves the present with alcohol and misery.

He usually comes back near midnight and blathers to my mother.

"They've ruined it all down there, Claire," he says. "You should see the mess they've created!" *They* being the poor black folk who moved in after white flight during the 1960's and 70's. My father has to blame someone for the bad things in life.

To him, *they* are just as good as anybody else to blame.

"All those beautiful homes," he says, shaking his head in a drunken, nostalgic sludge. "Burned down and abandoned. They're crack houses now! Hookers and bums all around! Can you believe that, Claire? *Fucking hookers!*"

I haven't seen the place in a while, but I imagine the old house looks like an ugly rotten tooth deteriorating from the inside out. During these nights, I sit in my bedroom with the lights off and wait for him to get home, my eyes adjusting to the dark, the headlights flashing through the window, creating a sigh of relief. Down the hall, my mother does the same in her bedroom, the carpet beneath her feet threadbare and beaten.

For being rid of testicular cancer, you'd think the old man would be happier, but he's not. He's more emotional and there's an incurable gloom in his speech, dark bags under his eyes like weak bruises. When I think about his missing testicle—the pink scar running across his crotch, the nubs of knotted skin—my tummy swirls like riding a roller coaster.

The doctors tried to prepare us. They pulled us aside and told us to expect a serious change in my father's behavior. But you can't prepare yourself to live with a man who suddenly doesn't care or have an interest in his family anymore.

Like my mother, I find it hard to swallow. I can't believe another person can ignore someone they supposedly love. In return, I try and ignore my father the way he's ignoring us. But that just makes me feel wrecked inside, guilty.

Later that weekend, I come home from a Saturday matinee to find my mother down in her basement studio, sitting on the floor and crumpled in a ball of despair. She's covering her face with her hands, which are stained dried-blood brown. Her paintbrushes are sitting in a mason jar, her palate mounted with dark earthy oils.

The vapor of an open bottle of turpentine stings my eyes like onion-smell.

"Mom?" I say to her, but she doesn't respond or even move. I can feel her hollowness in the pit of my stomach. I burn, my hands swelling into tightened knots. The telephone is lying in the corner of her work-space, broken and off the hook, the little springs and coils of the receiver sitting on the ground like little metal sea-creatures.

It's strange to see my mother crying in the middle of the day like this. She usually holds up until late at night when she goes to bed and cries herself to sleep, the space next to her empty and cold until the wee hours of the morning when my father slumps into bed.

"Mom?" I say. "Are you ok?"

Still she says nothing, and I wait for her to pull through. We sit in silence for what seems like an hour. Every few minutes, there's movement: a chuttle from her failing engine, a gasp, a wheeze, or she removes her hands from her eyes long enough to look into the full-length mirror nearby and see how beaten she is, or she glances at me and breaks down crying again, the tear ducts in her eyes getting dry like cotton seeds.

I want to erase all the aggravation that's been building up inside of her. She's ready to blow like a dysfunctional hot-water heater.

Out of nowhere, my mother gathers herself, as if just realizing I'm there. "Your father won't be home for dinner tonight again," she finally says through a muffled sob.

Dinner time. Women's boon of the 1950's. My mother still carries this responsibility like the indigestion from one of her pot roasts.

On my mother's canvas is an old wooden house in which she grew up, down in North Carolina. She's been painting the house from memory; the wood rickety, the porch falling apart. She now stares at the canvas, too, and I think perhaps she wants to return to North Carolina, just to get as far away from this life as she can.

I inspect the canvas closely. The wooden grain of the house has little faces in it, and it looks like they're huddling together in a group prayer, somberly whispering to God. The faces are asking Him to make the wood new again, to make the beams sturdy once more, the paint thick and protective. But God is stubborn. Same as always.

This is the day after the first time my father does not make it home at all from work.

At dinner two weeks later, things unravel a bit more.

As per usual, my father goes out every single night. He carouses and drinks and tries to prove his manhood to anyone who doubts him. His absence from home is now routine, and both my mother and I have stopped waiting up for him. I sleep throughout the night and dream about clogged toilets and leaky pipes.

My father goes out by himself or sometimes he calls a few high-school buddies. More and more, though, he's been enjoying the company of a lady-friend who teaches at the elementary school with him. This worries my mother. She thinks a broken home is the worst punishment in the world. But, unlike my father, she doesn't know whom to blame.

She doesn't have a *they*.

"So what are you and *Maureen* doing tonight?" my mother says. She's clutching a tea glass filled with tap water. Her silverware is perfectly placed and untouched.

To my father, this line of questioning is underhanded, sneaky. It's an invasion of his much-needed and well-deserved solitude.

"Come on, Claire," he says and rolls his eyes. My father is a beefy fellow with hair like the underside of an uprooted tree. Such antics, like rolling his eyes or scoffing, aren't quite right coming from such a large and intimidating man.

My mother picks up her napkin and dabs her clean mouth, though she hasn't eaten a bite. "Can't I ask what my husband is doing these days? Don't I have a right to know?"

"Don't give me that bullshit!" The old man points his fork at her. "I know what you're insinuating. We're just friends and you know it!"

It's a rare occasion for my father to even be home for dinner these days, and as much as my mother doesn't want to capsize our rickety life raft in paradise here, she's obviously concerned. She's been dreading an affair for days now.

I know my father isn't the kind of person to have an affair. I don't really understand what he's been going through lately, but he's totally incapable of cheating on my mother. He just doesn't have it in him. I'm not sure my mother understands this.

"It's not like that with Maureen," he continues, inspecting the puddle of spaghetti sauce on his plate. "She understands my situation."

"And I don't?"

"She almost died of breast cancer, Claire. She had a mastectomy. We're both missing something that used to be a part of us."

"That's an eloquent way of saying you're going out and drinking every night!"

Clearly my mother is pushing back, and that makes the spaghetti taste better. I actually do think she understands my father's loss, his reason to connect with somebody or something, like faith or his past or a psychiatrist. But connecting with another woman just hurts.

Thus far we've yet to approach my father about his behavior. We just watch him come and go because he looks so fragile, his bones thin like a windowpane. He's irritable. If I ask him how he's feeling, or ask him to help me out with the brakes on my bicycle, he becomes unhinged, and it's only a matter of time before he opens the door and never comes back.

Then I'll be a bastard.

I want to interject and tell my mother not to worry. But I don't want it to look like I'm defending my father at the dinner table. He's dug himself into this hole.

Besides, I'd met Maureen a week ago, and she certainly isn't someone you'd have an affair with. After a night at the neighborhood bar, she helped my father get home and up to the porch. The doorbell rang and there he was with this strange lady on the front steps. He was stinking drunk and she was bolstering him with her well-padded hip.

After Maureen steadied my father, she said, "Oh, you must be Steven," like she felt sorry for me. She was wearing green pants and had a huge bottom half that made her look like a monstrous pear with atrophied legs. She had fake, penciled-in eyebrows and a turkey gobbler underneath her chin.

"Yes," I'd said and looked at her chest. Underneath her blouse, I thought it must look like a bomb blew away her flesh, leaving the land charred and smoky.

"Is your mother home?"

"No, she's out."

"Oh, well, I'm Maureen."

"Hmmmgrrrppph," my father mumbled. He was peaked, on the

verge of puking.

"Is he all right?" I asked.

The old man opened his eyes and looked lost. It was like his body had someone else inside of it.

"Just get him to bed as soon as you can."

"Ok."

"And make sure he doesn't sleep on his back."

"Ok."

Like an unwanted package, Maureen handed my father over to me and then trundled off. He seemed heavier than a person of his size should be. I chalked it up to all that liquid sloshing around inside. I stumbled at the top of the stairs and almost lost him. I'd imagined his body rolling down the stairs, his head cracked open like an eggshell.

As I stripped off my father's clothes and rolled him over on the bed, I thought about taking a peek, inspecting his scar. But I passed. I wished my mother were home to confront Maureen. In the next few weeks, I was hoping there'd be a nasty catfight between the two, like the ones you see on the Serengeti on the Discovery Channel when food is scarce.

"Make sure I'm alive in a few hours, son," my father said to me before falling into an inebriated coma.

I was worried, so I called my older brother Paul up at Michigan State. His roommate told me he wasn't around and that he didn't know where Paul had been lately. But I knew Paul was there hiding behind a keg or something. My brother just didn't want to deal with what was going on at home. I didn't blame him. I heard the radio in the background and people cheering before he hung up. I felt helpless, alone.

After an hour, my mother came home. I rushed downstairs. "Dad's up in the bedroom passed-out," I told her.

"Is that right?"

My mother was beginning to care less and less about my father's whereabouts. Maybe a new defense mechanism she'd developed, thinking that if she didn't care or interfere, he might turn his life back around by himself and steer it in the right direction.

She'd stood, wondering if she should check on him. But she didn't. She went downstairs to her studio to paint. It was disappointing to see her so dead on the inside, but I couldn't blame her, either.

Around midnight, I looked in on my father, who was snoring loudly, twitching with every drawn breath. He looked in the midst of a very uncomfortable dream, but he was indeed alive.

My high school is in the same neighborhood as my father's elementary school, so when he isn't running late, he drives me to class in his busted-up mini-van. The early mornings give me a chance to see my father sober, alive.

"You doing all right in school?" he says, a steaming cup of coffee between his legs. I was waiting for the blackness to spill over the lip of the cup and scald his remaining testicle. I wanted that pain for him, just to remind him of what he's been doing to our family.

"Yeah, sure."

I stay short because I feel he doesn't deserve my attention.

"That McGratten character giving you any trouble?"

Mr. McGratten is my principal. Having worked in the same school system for so many years, my father knows every staff member in the district. It was hard for me to fuck up without him knowing about it.

"No."

"That guy used to give Paul hell," he says and digs deep into memory. "But that's just because he cared."

This is the first time in weeks my father mentions Paul, who has been steadily flunking his classes up at Michigan State. My brother had talked to me about dropping out and opening up a vintage baseball card store. It seems I'm the only one who cares about his circumstances lately. The old man can't seem to concentrate on anyone but himself. He doesn't chat with Paul when he calls, just passes the phone to me or my mother, if she's around and will listen.

Sometimes, when we're alone in his mini-van—beer cans lying in the front floor stinking with gnats, crumbs from drive-thru food on the dashboard—my father confides in me, though I feel he's holding back.

"I'm just living *my* life Steven," he says and thumps his chest. "I'm trying to make sense of what life even is. What if the cancer had been terminal? What if I was still in that hospital bed?"

I think about his would-be funeral, about my mother dating other men—men who have two testicles and don't hide inside of a bottle when times are tough. I think about Paul leaving school, taking over as the head of the family, getting a job in one of the automobile factories to make ends meet, dashing his dreams of opening his baseball card shop.

"I don't want to die without having a good time first. Is that so wrong?" he asks, fumbling with the radio knobs, finding some Smokey Robinson on the oldies station and snapping his fingers.

"I guess not."

I'm not really sure I want to be on his side. I'm not sure of anything, except I feel like crying as he snaps along to 'The Tears of a Clown.' Despite his plea for fun, my father isn't having such a good time. Like the drug commercials on TV, I decide we need to sit down and talk and find out what's going on in his life.

Before I get the chance to do that, he drops me off at school without even saying goodbye. The old man just taps the wheel and points at me as he sings along with Smokey.

On weekends, my mother and I go to a flea market called Gibralter Trade Center, which is a place where the dregs of southwest Detroit convene to sell absolute garbage to the public, all at a discount price. She sells her portraits and I help her set up the booth.

Gibralter has everything you don't want: mis-stitched Polo clothes, glowing posters of rainbows and unicorns, all the velvet El-vis' you could shake a stick at, neon Budweiser signs, handguns and shotguns and knives, gold by the chain, rare and hardly-used Stryper albums, broken vacuum cleaners and magical rug-cleaning products.

There *are* hidden bargains to be found in Gibralter, though most booths are complete scams. Most goods seem straight out of a 2nd grade "Arts and Crafts" disaster. These people slap a price tag on little Johnny's Styrofoam Easter Egg project and hope it sells, and even though I never see any actual transaction of money, weekend after weekend these poor souls come out and diligently set up their booths.

I'd like to believe my mother is different than these people. She's an artist with promising talent but stuck inside unforgiving circumstances. I feel bad we're condemned to such a place on a Saturday afternoon while my father is out doing God-knows-what. Still, she doesn't seem to mind we're here. We set up the booth and she pleasantly wastes the day by sketching, swirling her oils, dabbing at her canvas, and slowly drifting away into her own little world.

This is her therapy.

"I don't know what to do," she whispers while taking a break.

Having no answer, and not really sure that she's talking to me, I come up from behind and give her a soft hug. She pats my arms with those brittle fingers and says, "It's ok. It'll be ok." But I don't know whether she's saying this for her benefit or mine. "Oh how I wish I were painting on the seaside in southern France right now," she says dreamily.

I laugh and joke with her, trying to get a smile. "But you're stuck inside a dingy flea market on the south side of Detroit instead."

It probably stings her a bit, but she stays her course.

"Never give up on your dreams, Steven," she says and adjusts her easel, scrapes her palette with a palette knife.

This comes to me as hypocritical, yet so heartfelt that I cannot dismiss it. I can never forget she abandoned her artistry when Paul and I were born. She, too, has made her sacrifices in life.

I sit back down and watch my mother squeeze out paint from the tubes, her mind dull and worn. I can't decide whether she's a saint or an idiot for staying with my father, for coming to this flea-hole instead of mending her frayed marriage. It's not that she isn't trying to love my dad through all of this, but there's definitely a lack of effort.

In the end, I decide she's a saint amid the drone of a tattoo gun from across the aisle.

Early that following Sunday, after a quiet breakfast, my father gets dressed and opens the front door to leave.

"Can I go with you?" I ask from behind.

He stops dead in his tracks. Must be that he thinks his cruising is some sort of secret. It's better when it's a secret. He pauses at the door and then speaks with his back facing me, which is lumpy and tired. "You don't even know where I'm going, Steven."

"I do, too." I watch my father turn around, red-handed. "I want to go with you."

"Wear some work clothes," he says. "Meet me out in the garage."

Coming down the stairs half-dressed, my mother flashes me a glare from the kitchen sink. Her hands are sudsy from churning the dark dishwater over the breakfast dishes. She looks betrayed.

"I'm going with Dad!" I yell as I leave.

If she isn't going to try, I will.

My father is in the garage loading up a rake, a shovel and a cooler full of beer in the back of the mini-van. It's one of those sunny afternoons in late fall where the sky is clear and the air is sharp. The kind of day where nothing can hide. We have no secrets.

With a cold beer in his crotch, we back out of the driveway and head to Clark Park. We take Fort Street all the way up, the Ambassador Bridge looming in the distance, its rusty legs wading in the brown river. We take a few detours, tool around in the broken streets of Detroit. The cloudless sky makes my father open up a little.

"See that?" He points to an old building with a shipping dock overgrown with weeds and decay. "That's the old Keebler Distribution

Center. Before college, I delivered cookies to all the grocery stores on the west side." He drinks from his beer and points again, elated and proud. "And that's where your grandfather worked until the day he died."

We pass the vacant building with smashed out windows that look like broken teeth.

"It was an old tool and die shop. After work, he'd walk across the street there and sit on his barstool until it was time for dinner."

The bar is still there. It's called Norm's. A neon sign flickered in the greasy window.

"My mother would send me up to get him. Then we'd walk home together every night. Right down Hubbard Street here."

It's jarring to see my father live in this world. He's not recognizable. His face is bright like a bonfire. I imagine him walking down the street with my grandfather in the lazy evening, picking up a stick and dragging it along the fence, tossing stones in the gutter, carefree and full of hope. This is the first time in months I've seen my father truly happy.

Eventually, we pull up to my grandparent's old house, which looks terminally diseased, not even worth saving.

"Stay here a minute. Keep the car running just in case."

I get frightened, like we're robbing a bank. The old man jumps out as the dashboard buzzes and the keys in the ignition jingle. The back of the min-van slams shut and he approaches the front porch gripping the rake. Timidly, he looks into the front window, then knocks on the screen and yells: "Come on out you fuckers! Get the hell out of there!"

I lock the doors as my father attempts to scare out the bums with noise from the rake, slamming it repeatedly into the house and dragging it down the aluminum siding like a giant claw. He opens up the front door and then pauses to take a breath.

"Ahhhhhhh!" he yells and charges inside like a warrior.

Moments later, a handful of bug-eyed bums scatter out of the house like black sand crabs. Some are pulling up their pants, some are holding onto bottles of pink wine and swearing.

"Crazy white mother fucker!"

"What the hellzamatter with that guy?"

Confused and shaken, these men continue down the street and eye me curiously. All of them have dirt-brown eyes, and I can suddenly feel the difference between blacks and whites, years of hatred. It's awkward and distant.

My father tosses clothes and shoes and other debris out the front door. A few black ladies trickle out a moment later, half-dressed and disheveled. One of them is buttoning up her blouse while my father stands on the porch with his rake. Her bra is lacy and white.

"Get the hell out of here! And don't come back!"

When the coast is clear, I exit the van and we clean the house for the rest of the afternoon. It's hard work, but I do it with enthusiasm for some reason. I look at some of the black folks who pass by, wondering what the hell a couple of white people are doing here cleaning up this abandoned house. Occasionally, rats scamper out of from the dark cornices of the crawlspace and cobwebs silently attack our faces.

"I'm going to restore this house, Steven," he says proudly. "This is my neighborhood."

This seems too important to him, so I try to ruin it.

"But this isn't your neighborhood anymore," I say and point to the people on the street corner. "It's theirs."

After another week of my father's absences, some of the teachers begin calling the house. They're curious, nosy, and wondering if my mother is holding it together.

"Yes, I'm fine," she says into the receiver, a voice that resembles happy hour, fumbling with an aspirin bottle. "No, I haven't seen him in a few days… Yes, I'll tell him he missed the first night of Student-Teacher conferences. Thanks."

This is when my mother decides to leave. She loads up her car with a packed suitcase and slams the storm door shut, rattling my bones.

She honks the horn from the driveway until I come out of the house.

"Mom? What are you doing?"

"Just get your jammies and let's go, Steven," she says impatiently.

I pack some clothes in a duffel bag and wonder if my mother isn't overreacting.

We go to a hotel near I-75 in Southgate. Inside the room, I hear trucks on the highway rumble by on the wet pavement, hauling their trailers to factories and shipping docks into the barren streets of Detroit. The carpet deodorant tickles the back of my throat like a blast of pepper spray. The television is on but the volume is turned down.

My mother is soon on the phone, this time with a cigarette in her hand and a plastic cup of clear liquid stewing in a swirl of hotel ice. She hasn't smoked since she was pregnant with Paul. I've seen pictures. We don't blame her. It was a different time.

"I'm not going to sit around the house and wait for you, Greg," she says, takes a drag and nips at the liquid.

"Can I talk to dad?" I whisper. I want to ask him myself: Why haven't you been coming home?

But my mother shakes her head no.

I turn back to the TV and see a ticker tape run along the bottom of the screen: **WEATHER WARNING: A severe snowstorm warning for all of Wayne County. 6-8 inches expected.**

Tired of hearing my mother sob and swear at my father into the receiver, I leave the room and head down to the vending machines. I plug in some quarters and snag a bag of orange-colored potato chips. While watching the purple evening slowly overcome the day, I eat the tasteless chips and walk the perimeter of the hotel.

There are commuters and truckers unloading their belongings in the parking lot like a band of gypsies. There's also a noisy group of high-school seniors having a party in one of the rooms. I notice some of the students are from my school. Their door opens and closes many times and I hear bottles clank together and peals of laughter. They must have parents who despise each other too, or parents that don't care their kids are out drinking on a night like this.

Divorce is a contagious virus. Soon it will take over the world.

Heading toward the party is a bold move, and I feel nervous. I don't know why I'm going. I wasn't invited and I don't really know these people. But I can't stop myself. On one hand, I don't feel like being a part of this drunken masquerade, but there's also a part of me that wants to peek into someone else's life for a little while.

The gassy yellow light and noise wafts from the open door of the party and falls onto a fellow who is passed out in the open hallway, his bulbous head resting against the hotel banister, his mouth agape from all the booze and gravity.

I get the urge to pass out like him. I want to fall asleep without a thought in the world.

I step over the fellow's feet and look inside the room. It's a sad party. There are a few girls sitting on the edges of the beds, smoking cigarettes. They're chatting, blowing smoke into the air between their listless comments. There are also three guys standing by the beer chest near the bathroom in front of the vanity. All of them are wearing baseball hats, swaying with laughter.

I feel like I'm about to dive off the high-dive into a freezing pool of water. I step through the threshold of the door. Everything stops for a minute and I float. The girls look over at me and I stay still. Finally, one of them says "hello" and they all titter with laughter.

"Hello," I reply weakly.

After this, they go back to their quiet conversation, releasing me from my immobility. I head straight for the beer. The humiliation isn't so bad. I feel like the girls want me there. Fresh blood, a new element.

By the looks of the guards protecting the cooler of beer, though, I'm sure to get some resistance. But because they're so drunk, they just step aside and clear the way like an automatic garage door, not even acknowledging my presence.

"Excuse me—just gettin' a few beers," I say, nodding to a guy who has his back to the mirror. He's busy listening to one of the other guys talk about how drunk he had gotten the previous Friday. It's a big deal to brag about how much you can drink without ending up in the emergency room and getting your stomach pumped.

There's much laughter, like everybody in the world is having a great time. That's when I realize the fundamental difference between them and my father. These guys drink for fun—they don't really know any better. My father, on the other hand, drinks to forget.

Part of me wants to stay and drink for fun. I like their rosy faces and good cheer. But I feel awkward. I can't assimilate. Instead, I grab three beers and tuck tail out of the party.

I find an empty stairwell in the back of the hotel that faces the freeway. I sit down to drink the beers and think about what I can do to save my family. The clouds in the purple sky move in from the west like a determined infantry. The snow is coming, and it seems that—just like the situation with my father—there's nothing I can really do about it.

So I don't.

The metallic taste of beer lingers on my tongue and makes my mouth sour. I choke the first two down and watch the headlights on the freeway blur by. It looks like thousands of people fleeing the city because of the snowstorm. Or perhaps it's a thousand fathers ignoring a thousand wives, avoiding a thousand problems.

A few flakes of bright white snow begins to fall to the ground, creating a matted silence that crushes the world.

My father then walks around the corner of the hotel. He's holding a bloody hotel towel to his eye. The towel is packed with ice and looks like a butcher's apron after a hard day's work. The old man spots me and approaches. His gait is slow and labored.

I try to think of something to say. I want to say something meaningful, a few words that will change my father, make him come home and eat dinner with us the next day. But I stay quiet as he lumbers up the stairwell like a monster. I can't make this decision for him.

The old man sits down next to me with a contorted grunt and takes the rag away, a meaty knot of flesh protruding from his head.

"What happened to you?"

"Ahhh," he says, replaces the towel on his head, as if acknowledging the wound made it sting even worse. "Your mother caught me good with the telephone in the hotel room up there."

"You talked to her?"

"I thought I was getting through to her, but then she hauled-off and plugged me good with the receiver."

"Well, I don't blame her."

My parents have never been violent, and now I'm not so sure they'll be able to get back on the other side of that line. We sit in silence, my father's head drowsy and hanging low, the sound of the wet freeway traffic rushing by.

"Are you and mom getting a divorce?"

"No, your mother and I are not getting a divorce," he says confidently. "I'm just afraid, Steven. I can't deal with the situation."

I've never heard my father admit he's been defeated. His attention is then distracted.

"You got some beer there?"

I forgot that there's a full bottle and two empty ones at my feet, the beads of sweat running down the slender glass neck.

"What are you waiting for? Pop that thing open."

I crack open my first beer with my dad. I've heard stories about fathers sharing a beer with their son when they were old enough. To me, it's a fairy tale, it's some silly rite of passage for young men. This doesn't feel like one of those moments. He's simply out of beer and needs to have a drink, so he takes mine.

We share the beer while my father gathers his courage. He tosses back his head and almost finishes half the bottle. He hands it back and

I grip it like a lever and it feels like all I have to do is pull that lever back and we'll embark on a new life.

"You know, Steven…"

He stops and I give him the bottle, proffering the last good swallow. The old man finishes the beer, but not his sentence. It's disappointing, but the fact that he was even trying to explain makes me feel his commitment.

This man is my father.

"It's ok, Dad," I say. "Look, I'm going up to see Mom, all right?"

"Sure, sure," he says and he's still searching, wanting to say something profound. And I wait for one last moment and hope that he hasn't lost his focus entirely.

"Wait a minute," he says and hoists his body up, which is like watching a crane lift up a heavy, retired barge off the water. "I'm going with you."

I can tell he's reluctant. That he's still trying to grasp on to a world that gives him pleasure. But together we walk through the parking lot. As we do, I put my arm around him, to console his loss. Next to where the cars are parked, there is a large fence that separates the hotel and the freeway. Over the fence is a little stretch of concrete, which is littered with garbage, old tires and shopping carts.

My father straightens up, holds the beer bottle into the streetlight for a moment, making sure it's empty, then rears back and heaves the bottle over the fence. The bottle sails through the air, undisturbed and calm. It hits the cement on the other side and shatters. Both of us then climb the hotel stairs while the broken glass on the ground sparkles in the distance like moonlight across a dark lake.